THE MIDWIFE
OF TORMENT
&
OTHER STORIES

60 Sudden Fictions

ESSENTIAL PROSE SERIES 136

Canada Council   Conseil des Arts
for the Arts   du Canada

ONTARIO ARTS COUNCIL
CONSEIL DES ARTS DE L'ONTARIO
an Ontario government agency
un organisme du gouvernement de l'Ontario

Guernica Editions Inc. acknowledges the support of the Canada Council
for the Arts and the Ontario Arts Council. The Ontario Arts Council
is an agency of the Government of Ontario.

We acknowledge the financial support of the Government of Canada.

THE MIDWIFE
OF TORMENT
&
OTHER STORIES

60 Sudden Fictions

paulo da costa

GUERNICA
EDITIONS
TORONTO · BUFFALO · LANCASTER (U.K.)
2017

Michael Mirolla, general editor
David Moratto, interior and cover design
Cover / Back-cover Images / Drawings: João Ventura
Guernica Editions Inc.
1569 Heritage Way, Oakville, (ON), Canada L6M 2Z7
2250 Military Road, Tonawanda, N.Y. 14150-6000 U.S.A.
www.guernicaeditions.com

Distributors:
University of Toronto Press Distribution,
5201 Dufferin Street, Toronto (ON), Canada M3H 5T8
Gazelle Book Services, White Cross Mills
High Town, Lancaster LA1 4XS U.K.

First edition.
Printed in Canada.

Legal Deposit — First Quarter
Library of Congress Catalog Card Number: 2016952741
Library and Archives Canada Cataloguing in Publication
da costa, paulo, author
The midwife of torment & other stories : 60 sudden fictions /
paulo da costa. -- First edition.

(Essential prose series ; 136)
Issued in print and electronic formats.
ISBN 978-1-77183-162-8 (paperback).--ISBN 978-1-77183-163-5 (epub).
--ISBN 978-1-77183-164-2 (mobi)

I. Title. II. Series: Essential prose series ; 136

PS8557.A24M53 2017   C813'.6   C2016-905976-6   C2016-905977-4

To the misfits, oddballs, geeks, rebels,
eccentrics and outside-the-box thinkers
(who make this world wondrous)

Trago em mim o inconciliável e é este o meu motor.
I carry in me the irreconcilable, and that is my engine.
— **Pepetela,** *Mayombe*

———

Le secret d'ennuyer est celui de tout dire.
The secret of being a bore is to tell everything.
— **Voltaire, "Sixième discours: sur la nature de l'homme,"**
Sept Discours en Vers sur l'Homme **(1738)**

———

Those who don't believe in magic will never find it.
— **Roald Dahl**

CONTENTS

I: Affections

II: Slowness

V: Force

VI: Fathers

I: AFFECTIONS

BREAK-IN

Night falls.

The man switches off his desk light, slides behind his drapes and peeps at the apartment across the street. In the lit window, he follows the woman removing the obstacle course of school backpacks along the living room floor. The man eyes a wall painting, a ghostly train charging, full speed, across a high canyon's bridge. Above the abyss, on the tracks spanning the void, stands a sinewy body. Ears covered, back turned to the metal beast, a body screams. In the painting's frozen moment the man realises what is to follow is never conclusive. He longs to tell the woman now picking up toys scattered on the floor that she mimics that scream every time she steps on a piece of loose Lego; but he suspects she knows because she freezes even before she begins to scream, her mouth open, staring at the painting.

He can recite the steps of her life, the patterns, conscious, unconscious. In his business he cannot afford surprises. As usual, on Wednesdays, she had arrived at The Manor exhausted, dropping a trail of groceries from the bus stop to the foyer of the old building and yelling to her oldest boy to pick them up before he sneaked away to the elevator. In no time the boy could be found one storey above already planted in front of the TV for the evening.

The woman stands at the stove stirring an instant macaroni and cheese dinner. Her youngest sticks to her leg. The two older ones stick to the TV in the living room.

Mid-week and both sinks already crammed with pots, dishes and glasses, she walks out of view into the washroom to fill a jug with water, for juice. No clean dishes again. From the cupboard she brings out the last three paper plates. She will have to wait for one of the children to finish supper before she eats.

The children fed, she kisses them good-night, and collapses onto the sofa, a soggy paper plate in her hand. The TV still blaring, she stares at the silent scream hanging on her wall.

The woman wakes up with the first rays of sun entering the living room. The morning commotion begins, herding the children around the apartment, from bedroom to bathroom, from bathroom to breakfast, faster, faster, a missing sock, a mismatched outfit, in and out of rooms, mostly out. Scattered laundry grows in colourful mushrooming piles. The man already fears walking through the minefield of Lego and slippery macaroni. He'll wear rubber gloves and avoid fingerprints. The children are late for kindergarten, the woman is late for work, they abandon a half-eaten breakfast and she hurries out wearing excessive make-up and excessive jewellery to conceal her tiredness.

The oldest boy pretends to have forgotten his crayons, dashes, back into the apartment, and leaves one balcony door ajar to free the meandering cat. The cat thanks him, as usual, rubbing fur on his leg and settles in the sun inside the flower pot with the dead sunflower. Soon the cat will jump from the low balcony to explore the parking lot and locate the warmest car hood where he will lay for most of the day.

The man waits for their bus to arrive and disappear with the usual roar of lateness around the intersection. He runs down his building's staircase, crosses the street to arrive at the parking lot. He greets the cat. The entire day before him, he slides the rubber gloves on, and using the springboard of a car rack easily leaps over the balcony railings. For a moment he stops undecided, should he start with the dishes or the laundry?

CLOSER

Closer, the man encouraged, arm extended, fingers curled in a gentle domino tumble.

Standing by the door, the boy hesitated. Instead, he looked over the plush alligator clutched to his shoulder. Downstairs, from deep within the kitchen, the grave whispering voices, the smell of pizza and the clicking of glasses on the marble tabletop climbed the wooden staircase. He coughed a little, covered his mouth with the soft alligator jaws to muffle the sound.

I know, the man said, feigning a little cough himself, pointing his freckled nose in understanding toward the door. They just left. The doctor advised them I would be better off away from everyone. Especially from a certain snotty child, he added with a wink and a friendly smile.

The boy wiped snot trickling over his lip. He walked on tiptoes to the man's bedside.

I like my boy snotty anyway, the man said with a nod, a blink of the eyes.

The child smiled, relieved. Then he glanced over to the door again.

They will never know you were here.

Mother said I'm not allowed to come near you now.

I understand.

She said it's dangerous to play as we used to play. That you are a very sick person. She made me swear to it.

Yes, I understand.

The man and the child gazed awkwardly at each other.

But would you like to? The man opened his arms, leaving them open as a gigantic moth while making a cocoon, a space to embrace anything wishing to be embraced.

The child swayed his body, lowered his eyes and clung more tightly to his alligator. Moments passed and he again looked shyly at the man on the bed. Nodded.

The man offered his arm, again. His other hand patted the frayed velvet bed cover. This time the child clutched his hand, climbed the bed to his lap.

The man brought the tender face of his grandchild against his. Every breath of his life had been worth the journey to this moment, this last touch, the warmth of skin on skin. He did not want to leave this earth as a pestilence to be avoided by all. Some things in life were not worth preserving at this late stage to prolong time a worthless little longer. The child coughed a little, embraced him with the mighty small strength of his arms, not wanting even a whisper of air between them.

I miss you, grandpa.

I miss you too, Aiden.

Is it true they are taking you away?

The grandpa nodded, correcting: I am going away on my own.

A place where you'll get better?

The grandpa nodded again.

So that we'll be able again to play riding the horse?

I'll try.

Aware this would be the last time he would hold those silky hands, the man's chest tightened. He already missed the days when he would not wrestle with his grandchild, carry him on his shoulder or sit at the table with him on his lap pretending he was a tractor climbing the shifting, treacherous ground. At his ripe age touch became a rarity and children remained the ones offering him this elixir of life and asking for nothing in return. Through his grandchild he also travelled back to an age when his daughter had still embraced him with a clear feeling of surrender that pressed their love into every pore of skin.

He could die happily in the arms of this child smelling of angels. He found no vacillation in the love of a child. The purity and limpid emotion was a balsam to any sickness.

The child coughed.

He drew the deep breath of his demise. He kissed the child. He smelled the earth after a snowfall. Fresh. The smell of a pharmacy. The younger breath smelled of one who had yet to swallow death in the corpses of animals at the table and in the countless hurts of the heart.

Aiden.

Noses nearly touching, the boy looked into his eyes.

Grandpa, your breath still smells like the compost bucket.

Oh ... I'm sorry, the man said covering his mouth.

I still love you, the boy said nodding fiercely to leave no doubt. Then he paused to evaluate his words further. The compost not so much.

The man smiled. Promise me something, Aiden.

Yes.

Whatever happens, never tell your parents you were in this room.

The child nodded.

Remember, I was the one who called you in. There is nothing wrong in giving your grandfather a hug. There never was, and there never will be. And after today nothing that may happen to me will be your fault. None of it. Do you understand?

The child nodded, biting his lower lip.

You know your grandfather loves you more than alligators love the swamp, don't you?

The child nodded and stared at the alligator squeezed between them.

I love you and I always will. Wherever I'll be.

Will I see you again?

In your dreams, your memories. Whenever you want to.

Can I cuddle and lie next to you?

Only for a minute, this time.

When the boy returned from his aunt's, after a week recovering from his pneumonia, he walked up the stairs to his grandfather's empty room. A strange new smell in the house infused the curtains, the door knobs, burned his nostrils. Every window ajar, yet the breeze sweeping the air appeared powerless to erase that smell.

Clinging to his alligator, crouching inside his grandfather's closet, searching for the compost smell he so missed, the boy overheard his mother's voice climb up the staircase from the kitchen and telling his aunt.

We don't understand. He knew at his ripe age that any contact with the child would be fatal. Still, he refused to be sent away from the kid if only for a little while. He had promised to warn us anytime the child wanted near him so we could stop it. They were so close.

THE WAIT

You walk out. You walk out as if you had no plans to return. I say no, don't go. I say it in the only way I know: a sigh and a lowering of the eyes. That triggers a guilty glance over your shoulder, followed by irritation because you know you must leave me.

I press my nose against the window glass. My longing tracks you to the car while you avoid my eyes and disappear. I don't move. I hear the distinctive growl of the car engine above the city roar. Soon the TV, left on out of pity, drowns the faint echo of your heart. Trancelike, I stare out the window, hoping.

Who do you think you are? Telling me you love me, telling me no one understands you like I do. Telling me lies. Don't you know I would die without you? Die everyday a little? No, you don't know.

After an eternity of boredom, the sun disappears, and I hear the whine of your car engine. On seeing me, you wave, as if I had never moved and you had never abandoned me. I wave back. No one, but no one, runs to you like I do, starved after a day of emptiness, dropping everything to greet you. From room to room, I follow your every step. I cannot bear the separation, I cannot bear to miss a single crumb of attention.

Who do you think you are to keep me on a leash so I don't leave you like your last lover? What would I do without you? You complain to me. I don't judge. I don't interrupt. I do whatever you ask me to do. No questions asked. I don't inflict the insults your daughter does. I sleep with you. You cry to me. I see you naked and ask for nothing.

PLEASANT TROUBLES

A sudden, involuntary flaring of his tongue, a hideous contortion of his face; and apart from this peculiar affliction, Bonifácio Careta remained an ordinary child. The villagers believed everyone entered life with unique, God-given graces — some born to nose-picking, others to continuous spitting, others to limping. They never spent a second thought on Bonifácio.

Bonifácio Careta's life would have proceeded without remarkable attention if misfortune had not brought his peculiar condition to public notice.

Bonifácio's fortunes changed irrevocably on the occasion of the long-awaited Papal tour of the country with the Pontiff's brief, unscheduled outhouse stop in the boy's forgotten village. While the Pontiff bestowed upon the gathering crowd his holy blessing, his Holiness' finger fell with singular exactitude upon the unsuspecting Bonifácio. Drawn to Bonifácio's angelic face, his perfect, clustered freckles and pleasant manners, the radiant smile that could distract buzzing bees from their business, His Sanctity curled his finger and summoned the boy.

Brought forward, the Pope kissed and blessed the boy.

"Little angel, would you like to come with me and join the priesthood?" the Pope enquired, patting Bonifácio's buttocks. Bonifácio's affliction flared and his tongue stuck out half a metre. The Pontiff, shocked, blessed himself and the child. "May our souls be safeguarded from the devious ways of Satan," he said, attempting to push the child's tongue back inside his mouth. Bonifácio did not know about Satan, he only knew his tongue carried a mind of its own. Without warning, it would dart out in the manner of a deranged clockwork cuckoo, wreaking havoc in the predictable world outside. Then his muscles would stiffen and no force or fancy could return the tongue to its proper place.

Sales of papal icons and newspapers doubled after the Pope's "*face to face encounter with the devil*," as the inflammatory press headlined the event along with a photograph of Bonifácio's pinkish tongue. The villagers began to believe Bonifácio Careta cursed. They prayed novenas. Masses were sung. His mother, Alzira, crawled on her knees the entire way to the miraculous Lady of Fátima, seeking Her intercession for her son's affliction.

When the prophets of science arrived, they promised Bonifácio a cure. And indeed, the scrutiny of a scalpel quelled his tongue's random flaring, a noticeable improvement, but soon after, it hung out in the world for hours at a time, creating another nuisance. By grace, the cure proved temporary.

At first, if anyone had inquired, Bonifácio would have admitted to enjoying the sudden pink extrusions, as no other soul could boast such a tongue. He looked forward to the astonished reactions. After the continuous efforts to mend and improve him failed, he succumbed to popular pressure, and thought himself sick, evil, tormented.

Children taunted him during the school's lunch break. "Hey, lizard tongue! We've brought you lunch!" and they laughed, dangling dead flies in his face, tempting his tongue. In despair, Bonifácio hid himself, held a knife to his lips, prepared to end the agony. His tongue, knowing better, refused to exit.

The unforgiving village would have Bonifácio finish his days in freak shows for public amusement, if it were not for the village *curandeira*, Felismina. Felismina did not believe the pointed accusing fingers, did not believe him in bondage to a torment. Instead, she advised Bonifácio to disregard the whispering, the finger-pointing, and encouraged him to embrace his uniqueness.

"Your tongue is not terrible. Remember when it flared during Sunday communions!" she said. Bonifácio half-smiled remembering Father Lucas, who for lack of a better course of action, fed him host upon host to appease the insatiable demon inside. Nevertheless, in Bonifácio's eyes the tongue caused him more trouble than pleasure.
"I'll reveal the hidden gold of your tongue," Felismina assured him. "Come visit me Sunday morning after mass."

Bonifácio walked up to the meadow where wild flowers bowed to the morning breeze and the sweet fragrance of wild honey hives perfumed the air. Felismina sat on a boulder, in front of her stone-hut, eating wild strawberries gathered in her lap. She blindfolded Bonifácio and led him through the undulating meadow where he learned to distinguish a lily from a lady's slipper, and a harebell from a marigold by the delicacy of their pollen melting on his tongue.

As the years passed Felismina taught Bonifácio to concoct exotic oils from the wild flowers' flesh and instructed him in the art of touch. Bonifácio's innate virtuosity awakened. He caused a sensation among the village girls, prompting him to be elected as the most handsome man in the village despite his zigzag nose and oversized ears.

Under Felismina's guidance Bonifácio established a reputation for his tongue's divine abilities. An oracle, it flagged omens of the matrimonial future. For such gifts, brides in the surrounding area visited him the night before their weddings, eager for an accurate prediction of their married lives. And they returned with radiant smiles to confirm his fame. The news spread. Widows and married women found miraculous cures for their apparent terminal discontent in their faithful weekly visits to Bonifácio. The village grew joyous with the boy's metamorphosis of curse to nurse, and Bonifácio found his place well before History found him.

WHEN THE DEAD
REFUSE TO DIE

Considering the woman Dona Branca had been and the enemies she had sown in life, I'm surprised at the number of mourners around her coffin. After the devilish tricks she pulled on me, I, for one, don't know why I'm here. But we're all children of God and dying's dying no matter who you were and how you lived. Even the devil deserves a decent burial.

Seeing Dona Branca so still and silent now, it's hard to remember her spitting out the wrongs with everything in sight, unnecessarily banging the door as she entered my grocery store, complaining of dust here, rotten smell over there in the apple corner and flies everywhere, god help me. On Saturdays, wanting oranges, and obstinate, refusing to buy the ones on the shelf: "Won't touch something half the neighbourhood's already groped, oh my." Suggesting that I hid the immaculate fruit, the juiciest, elsewhere out of sight. A customer may be stupid or ignorant or rude, but a customer's always right. So, I'd scurry down the cellar stairs to haul up a fresh box for her to grope through at her leisure, while I watched her smelling each fruit's belly button for ripeness, waiting and taping my foot until she settled on the single one she would buy. And that's how I earned my hernia.

Look at the overabundance of flowers in the room. In

light of the nuisance she made of everything, it's hard to imagine that many souls in the village who cared. And the village children? Look at them, grown up now showing off snotty seedlings of their own. Two crops of rascals chased by Dona Branca's broom for trampling the forget-me-nots lining the public fountain, for playing too loud too late, for climbing trees not to be climbed. Wonder what the children will do now without Dona Branca to harass?

Even Gregório Batabranca, the village pharmacist, pays his respects in his angelic white uniform. Least he could do. After all, he counted her among his stellar customers. Sure helped him pay for that marble palace of a home. Dona Branca should have been spending her mornings in the fresh air with the bricklayers, helping them mix the concrete and getting some exercise while at it. Better remedy for her obesity in the end, I'd say. A born complainer, always an ache here, an ache there. The liver mostly. It's common knowledge that more than once she returned Gregório Batabranca's prescription. The bottle label claimed a hundred pills and she counted ninety-nine.

I can't believe my eyes, Osório Ossos, the grave-digger, crying as he shuffles past her open coffin. Surprising. After she complained to our priest about the infested state of God's garden, Osório Ossos almost lost his job. I'll bless myself and kiss the cross if I didn't hear Osório yell in mass, that the weeds weren't his problem. He blamed the fertilizer. People's caustic bodies leaking into his soil, just like the thoughtless lives they had cultivated before dying. And as he stomped away, he gave Dona Branca's ears a last ringing: he would dig her six feet deep when her turn came and she wouldn't have to worry about weeds, her plot would be too poisoned to grow even a measly stinging nettle.

I can't believe I let them dress her in that pink polyester blouse. Regardless of what they say, the silver painted fingernails still suit Dona Branca's perm best. Looking at the restful body, one almost forgives her mean-spirited soul, sticking her nose into everyone's business, leaving nothing for Sergeant Bolota to do. The poor man, blowing his nose so loud now, he parrots an angel's trumpet. Mourning for his lost holidays, I suspect.

The day Dona Branca told Sergeant Bolota that road signs were as useless as the written law, I sat cross-stitching, on my front steps, across from the police station. The sergeant ignored Dona Branca. He rocked on a wicker chair outside his post, tooth-picking, listening to a soccer match on the radio glued to his ear. Weekend drivers accelerated past our doors in their cars, raising clouds of dust.

"Sergeant, you are no good in keeping law and order," she insisted, having brought a rose under his nose for inspection. "I can't keep a proper garden, if you don't keep up your end of the law on this street."

The sergeant stared at the sad rose, dulled under a mantle of brown filth.

"The faster they drive, the less dust they'll raise, Dona Branca," Sergeant Bolota grumbled, pushing away with his thumb the rose tickling the curled hairs in his nose.

Dona Branca wouldn't have appreciated this much noise, even less at her funeral. Young children don't belong at funerals. Such racket. I'll ask the mothers to leave if they don't have the decency themselves. Damn them all. I'm her next door neighbour and she died confiding in me. Did that little rascal kick me on purpose when I herded him and his mother out? I only twisted his ear for prevention. Can't let them get away with stealing an orange or they'll swipe your whole grove next time around, that's what Dona Branca would have said and justifiably so.

The procession is late. This coffin will never leave this bottleneck unless I do something. Gee, if everyone in here would just hurry up with their mumbling prayers and shelved-off their curiosity about who she left her money to — money said to be hidden under the mattress where she lies — and if others stopped chatting and whispering while conducting their private business with disrespect for her dead body and allowed instead the patient souls lining up outside their turn, then we might move this circus along. I'll elbow my way through the mob of people toward the coffin where the priest stands and tell him he ought to close the lid and begin this procession because even the poor need to rest. Goodness gracious, let the dead at last die.

THE RED VINEYARD

Yesterday, the day before unveiling our hardened up labour to the judgement of the world, and mostly of his patron, our Master erased Günter from the vineyard, replacing him with a dull horse pulling a cart of grapes. It sent shivers of repugnance throughout the labourers in the painting.

We were not fazed by such intimidation. After Master wrapped the canvas in the finest Amsterdam linen, in the hope of appealing to the droll taste of his patron, we went to rework History behind the scenes. We began by carting the stagnant water from the river and washing off the top layer covering Günter. We placed him where he belonged. This time, he will stand in the river, doing nothing, apart from casting a long, long shadow and finally stretching his bones. We hope the message is clear. We took pity on the horse whose fault to be in the scene was not his and let him be. We also smudged our faces not to be identified in our eternal smirk.

This morning, with only air in his decanter and not even a mouldy crust in his bread basket, we overheard Master confide to a trusted female friend that we were creations beyond his control. We had to laugh. Luckily, we were bending toward the vines and our impertinence went unnoticed. As usual our Master's eyes turned ablaze, a feverish possession of divinity as though he was privy to God's table, as though a mystical deliverance from the heavens had instructed his hands, and he simply obeyed the command. Painters tell stories to sell their indulgences and visions of madness in exchange for bread and twice as much burgundy. No regular folk can afford to fall prey to fantastical stories of inspiration by those who believe they are the chosen ones, appealing to your awe. If Master truly allowed the scene to paint itself, tell its own story, and if his hand indeed merely followed the wishes of the people wanting to be born, he should have known Günter wanted to stay playing his flute quietly by the water's edge. The poor man was not bothering the flies or frogs and had already laboured fourteen hours that day as proven by the setting sun. All along, Frida also had wanted her skirt maroon frilled in yellow lace. Franz had begged for a gourd of water. Anke just wanted to be home with her baby.

This unkempt Master, splattered with paint up to his surly hair, does not understand what the viewing public desires. For some time now, since he lost his ear, he has been stuck in the shivering cold blues of blurred flowers. Considering we are the ones watching the eyes of the gazer upon us, we know where their eyes come to rest. It is always the yellows, reds and oranges. Flesh, body parts, blood, missing limbs. So last night we took a break from the back-bending labour of the grape harvest and decided, for once, to please the viewer and offer them what they wanted.

Change was of course an arduous decision, made more difficult to implement once you were glued to your own history and the image of yourself. The canvas that framed us ended at the borders of our life time, meaning that to walk from one border to another required unstickily stubbornness from each of us. We knew the price. The most vicious responses would arise from those accustomed to what you were. They would resist the change. They would rather destroy you than encourage the different reality they would be catapulted into by the shifted expectations.

We were not naïve. Once you were caught together in a painting it was for eternity and a half. We were not willing to stand idle before the prospect of perpetual neglect in a dusty corner, likely eaten away by mildew and moths. Frida already suffered terribly from her allergy to oils, and the prospect of her unstoppable sneezing through the centuries, not offering a deserved rest to the remainder of us wrapped in the dark and clacking our teeth in a stored away collection, became sufficient impetus to send everyone in the vineyard bleeding across the canvas for change. We knew that to save ourselves from oblivion required a rewriting of our history. For years now, Master has wondered why he failed to make a splash on the scene. There would be no splash to be seen until we had finished our most important labour in the course of last night, a labour of love concealed under the most expensive linen of Amsterdam.

The clanking of footsteps entered the room ahead of the swish of long robes lifting the crusty dust on the creaky floor boards. In our vineyard not even a leaf on the vines swayed. The fish in the river stopped jumping and the undercurrent running. We held our breath; Frida placed her hand over her nose for precaution.

The linen slipped to the ground in a swift swoop. We were not looking at Master. The deadly silence and the wide open jaw painted the words in his mind. We focused on the patron and our future. The one with the yellow coins jiggling in his pockets cannot create anything but his approving smile could ensure more of the golden music in Master's pocket.

We sighed when the loud burp echoed in the room and the wine began flowing into chalices. Master fell to his knees rubbing his eyes in disbelief for all the distortions, smudges and waves in the strokes of the brush. Regardless, he accepted the full chalice without protest.

We were the last ones to laugh.

LONG RUN

He jogs along the river valley dappled in Autumn hues. The sun hides behind the stone curtain of the Rocky Mountains. In different company he might consider this moment romantic.

"I'll swat you if you move any closer. Nothing personal. You remind me of a buzzing dentist's drill and a prickling syringe, all in one." He breathes in gasps as a result of his steady pace.

"I understand. Nothing personal either."

After sitting cross-legged for the past mile, buzzing into his ear, the mosquito lifts off from his shoulder. She lands on his bare arm, the softest part, where a needle will penetrate with ease. She means business. Not well versed in Gandhi's passive resistance or in conflict resolution, he swings his arm, slaps hand against flesh. The mosquito escapes between his fingers, laughing. He stares at the welt.

The mosquito lands on his nose and he decides not to attempt anything brusque this time. From this perspective she looks all legs. He prays for fate or a sudden gust of wind, to resolve this unpleasant encounter. He believes in divine interventions.

She persists. "Come on, be a sport. I'm counting on your

co-operation to bear children. It's my biological clock. Not my fault, really."

He has never heard it reasoned with such straight-forward finesse before. Quickening his pace, he searches the sky for a guiding star. The overcast evening reveals no omens and hides a lucky constellation. All he sees are legs tap dancing on the bridge of his nose.

"It won't take long, I promise," the mosquito says; runs her needle along his flesh; pretends to press here and there; flutters at the prospect of warm pulsating blood.

"I hate needles," he says shuddering. Annoyance fuels his stride.

Jogging allows him to escape daily troubles, losing track of them on the long run. But now he faces someone with just as much stamina and far better endurance.

He glances at his chronometer. At this frantic pace he will break his personal best. The thought comforts him, and even more comforting will be breaking the news in the office.

"We could finish this business in a single instant and save ourselves the trouble of foreplay. You know you can't sleep with me buzzing around your mind."

The man arrives at the back gate to his house and shifts from leg to leg, weighs the fear of the needle, weighs the annoyance of an all-nighter versus a fly-by-night.

"About the children, would I be involved in their up-bringing?" He dreads obscure long-range commitments. Bad practice in business or love. "Will they hang around my yard?" he adds with a sigh of concern, inspecting the im-maculate green lawn, the symmetrical chairs around the wrought iron table keeping company with the glimmering barbecue.

The mosquito circles his head, flying closer and closer to his ears. Agitated by the annoying buzz, desperate, he swings his arms in the air. His shallow breathing quickens. He steps into his backyard. She follows.

"All right, your place then!"

He jogs back to the river valley. He agrees to her request on the condition that the little mosquitoes carry his last name.

She lands on the white flesh, while short of breath, he looks the other way.

CLOSET OF MEMORY

I don't know why my eyes sprang up from the black asphalt, from my deflated bicycle tire, at the precise moment she strolled past. Our eyes paused, connected. I remember her long cream dress buttoned at the front, her lips rosy of their own. Something inviting about her emerald eyes that suggested bliss, a promise, an inevitable abandonment to the torture of day after day of not knowing more and longing for everything; eyes lost in the world of someone else's face.

With religious discipline I revisit the cracked patch of black asphalt where dandelions have since sprung up. I sit, watch wind part the long grass in wavering irrational lines. I cradle a novel. I collect pebbles scattered at my feet and rearrange them into a heart shape. Every time a pastel silhouette fills the horizon, I lick my finger, open the book at random, and pretend to be immersed in the plot. Out of the corner of my eye I register my disappointment and tear out another page. The book and my holidays are nearly finished and I never left the city park by the river at the end of my street. I should shoot a few photos of my holiday to show back at the office.

At night, I stroll up and down the street leading to the park. I peek into windows. Sometimes I climb fences. I pray that my escapades won't inflict a heart attack on one of the elderly. Or the-not-so-elderly. Everyone carries a vulnerable heart.

Another fruitless night of wandering the streets, I return and climb into bed with her detached eyes pacing through the darkness of the room. I can't imagine their colour in the darkness. What if I don't recognise her now even if I see her? I remember her long cream dress, still buttoned at the front, hanging like a ghost in the closet of my memory.

I snuggle closer to my partner and kiss him on the nape of his neck. He stirs. Early morning rays stream through the bamboo blinds. Without opening his eyes, he turns and whispers warm thoughts in my ear: "This Spring obsession is taking longer than usual!" He curls up to me, rests his hand on my chest. "When you find her, bring her home," he adds. "Nothing should stop a new love from renewing an old one."

NOT A MARRIED KISS

It was not a married kiss. Not a kiss the man could anticipate from years of practice. Without surprises. A married
kiss he could count on. Sustaining, wholesome, good for
him, taken for granted every Friday after boiled potatoes
and whittling.

It was not a married kiss, but a kiss that blossomed on
the flower of his lips, exploding in a maddening tingle of
orange nectar whetting his mouth, tinting his imagination.
It was most certainly not the domesticated kiss, tasting of
water, innocuous, ready to drown new untameable fires.

The man's wife preferred he did not go around kissing.
Didn't all the kissing between them give birth to Brian? She
feared losing her husband the way she had lost her son, who
disappeared with a duffel bag over his shoulder after his
first Valentine kiss. The shower of motherly kisses had been
insufficient to immunize him. Through the backyard window she followed the dance of a butterfly fluttering from
flower to flower, none unwilling, none disappointed. In
truth, she lost Brian the day she delivered him to the world
of lips wanting to taste and be tasted.

THE WALL MOVER

In a theatrically-stern voice the father warned his four-year-old he must be careful. "Superboy Rocco might grow so strong from his nightly practice of pushing walls out of his way, that one day he might indeed push the bedroom wall over and bury us under the rubble. You know, a house needs a wall like a baboon needs the balloon." The boy laughed, pretended to be already trapped under an imaginary wall of stone, begged his father for rescue. The father indulged his son's play, struggling with dramatic emphasis as he reached the stretched hand of his son and pulled him to the safety of a cuddle against his chest. The boy giggled.

The following evening during his Superboy play acting, wall-pushing, bedtime ritual, the long feared earthquake of the millennium assailed the coastal region, and the wall, as well as the rest of the house, shook for an interminable minute. The boy clenched his teeth and pushed the wall with added eagerness in the face of his unexpected success. He laughed with hysterical gusto, enjoying one more of the many surprises his father often introduced to their games, never a dull moment. In his child's mind the boy deepened the adulation for his father's powers who this time had outdone himself. At that instant, his father acted to perfection his terror of the Superboy power-shaking the house, the windows, the furniture, and he fell off the bed in a panic.

When the rescue crews reached the house a day later, they discovered the boy still feebly calling after his father to free him, and that he was tired of the game, and that never again would he play Superboy with such an important matter as a house wall. And why was papa not saying a word for so long? Was he mad at him for bringing the house down? And were his sister and mother also upset at him?

The boy lived the rest of his life on the streets and beaches, the urban woods and parks, and as far away from a wall as feasible in a city. He lived with his pet turtle Panquelim which had survived the earthquake in the shelter of its shell and, determined, had crawled among the debris to sit by the boy's face, eating the dust from his lips and licking the salt from his tears.

To this day, even in rain, Rocco prefers the shelter of a tree canopy, blaming himself, not only for the death of his father, but convinced he had caused the earthquake that had killed seventy-five thousand. You may see Rocco in your early morning walk to work as he rolls up his foam mat and wool blanket on a park bench; he will lower his gaze to the ground to avoid yours, ashamed of the harm and pain he has caused, for he knows no one was left untouched by the tragedy of his foolish childhood dream coming true.

A PERFECT
AND PLEASANT DAY

He pedals with gusto. On a cycle tour through the cobblestone roads of the grape-growing French countryside, he notices the speed with which he has fallen out of shape after a chaotic week at the office and his late martini bar evenings. The grade is gentle; mostly rolling hills. Country folk, watering their flowers, wave as he passes. He waves back. Fall is his favourite season. Tinged burgundy, the vine leaves warm his eyes. A soft breeze cools the air. He plans to work up to his top-notch form and ride the Pyrenees at the height of summer.

This is the first outing in his long-range goal to enter *Le Tour de France*. He squeezes the water bottle, douses his face while the breeze picks up. He breathes at length the fragrance of ripe grapes.

His telepathic cellular rings inside his head. He matches the frequency.

"Honey, I'll leave dinner ready for you. Escargots à la Provençale and Crèpe Suzette. Will 9 be okay? I'm off to Cleopatra my nose and deepen my tan for the theme party at the Al-Fadin's next weekend."

Always thoughtful, Tanya programmed the meal with culinary fare to match his cycling goal. He feels complete.

"And honey, I'll leave one of our favourite conversations cued and ready to go. Feel free to browse through my clothing file and dress me in something nice to suit your mood. Now be careful, the roads are treacherous!"

In a pleasant French accent, his wrist computer reminds him that his session is about to expire. He removes the hi-resolution goggles, deactivates the breeze, empties the aroma diffuser and jumps off the exercise bike. He returns "The Vineyard Tours of France" disc to the gym's front desk winking at the receptionist. "Won't be long before I'll be signing out the real thing," he says, pointing at the *Le Tour de France* disc on the shelf behind her. Polite, she smiles back.

He sighs, a peaceful, satisfied sigh, and before he steps onto the street, he fits a gas mask over his face.

THE MUG AND THE PARAKEET

The woman wanted to paint the living room. After all, it had been some time since they freshened it up last with a new bright coat.

"It needs to be retouched," she insisted, one hand caressing the other.

Reluctant, the man lowered the newspaper, diverted his attention from the horse-racing section. Glancing at the wall, he noted nothing of concern. The paint appeared fine. Yes, he conceded the existence of a few smudges around the light switches, and black stains where the bookshelf rubbed the wrong way against the wall. It was nothing that a proper scrubbing could not settle.

"It's been so long," she pleaded, wringing her hands, before picking up her mug of coffee and taking a last sip of the bitter liquid.

"I'll worry when drywall crumbles or a stud shows," he replied, eyes riveted between the lines of the newspaper. "It's perfectly fine," the man concluded and flipped the newspaper to the next page.

The woman hurled the mug. It grazed the man's ear, exploding on the wall behind him, jolting the man from the weather report page forecasting sunshine and an end to wind storms. The mug shattered, sending a thousand porcelain slivers travelling into the parakeet's cage. The parakeet halted the chirping of a song.

"Oops, it slipped," the woman said, before the guilty hand covered her mouth, a twinkle in her eye.

A beige skin of paint had peeled around the fist-size crater on the wall, and the woman, encouraged by the instant change on the living room landscape, dreamed of painting it over in vibrant colours. No more of the dull, depressing beige that encircled the crazy house where she no longer could distinguish between the tamed man in his beige shirt and the imprisoning living room wall. Was he part of the daily background or had he disappeared into the pores of the wall? Vermillion. Yes, vermillion, the woman decided with purpose.

The woman swept the porcelain slivers onto the dustpan and sent them away for burial in the municipal waste dump. A day later, the parakeet died, leaving the beige house in sepulchral silence. Puzzled, both man and woman wondered what had killed the bird and silenced the music in their home. The nearly invisible sliver of porcelain that sank through flesh, that tore into the bird's heart, remained concealed for eternity.

Despite the woman's continual longing for vermillion, despite the new absence of a shared song to overwrite the cutting disquiet of newspaper pages turning at every breakfast, the hole in the wall was never refilled.

HER LONELINESS THE DOG

Loneliness is the unbearable scent of your damp hair clinging to my bed quilt, heat vents, my velvet sofa. Vacuuming for the third time this Sunday morning, thick black hair, still growing out of the table's legs, snags my toes. Why does death leave cold traces? Sadness roots in untouchable memory. Red eyes. Last Friday evening no tongue wetted my face, leaping from the front steps as I opened the door to a weekend not in each other's arms. No weight on my lap, drooling and listening or a comforting heavy sigh while I would recount the uphill moments of my day.

The refrigerator sounds unusually lively now, growling and gurgling against the morning silence, watching me pace back and forth to your photo on my night table and the candle burning. In the blown-up photo above the bed, your tongue droops.

I decide on fresh air, step onto the porch and automatically reach for the leash. Memory pulls my hand, caresses your thick coat of fur, and almost voices: let's go. I walk twice a day to the supermarket. Wander the aisles and find something or other to carry back. Find a use for my hands. I cannot squeeze another carton of milk in the overflowing fridge. I avoid the top of the bluff where we raced side by side, seasons of light and dark, wet and dry, tempest and calm. Yesterday, I strolled, hands in pockets, clasping the leash to a fist, hood over my face, as old, dog-named acquaintances walked past me. Fluff, the mountain terrier trotting ahead of his grey-whiskered dad. Maila, the grey-hound, on the heels of her thin-faced owner.

Overlooking the river, I stop, shift from leg to leg, and listen to past echoes of brief encounters on the ridge.

"How's Fluff doing today?"

"Fluff had a great day. Fluff would be pleased to invite Bess for a long walk at Nose Hill Park next Saturday night."

Shifting from leg to leg. Throwing a stick.

I am at the pet store gazing at a Newfie again.

None with the adorable white splash on the tail's tip, matching her left paw. Considering the possibility of bleaching the puppy's tail white. Walking away in a fluster. In my mouth the same taste as when I went to the bar the day after my husband died.

The best boyfriends, since then, dropped on their feet and wrestled, fought you for the chewing bone, growling and pawing, giggling and rolling. The others, of which there is no history, they could not share our bed or listen to a daily summary of your diatribes before the expected sex, and alas their dreams of a future slipped through the cracks of their silence even before the arrival of morning.

Again dreaming of you Bess, I wake up breathless, a heaviness sinking my heart as if you had your paws on my chest. My wet, cold face, not from your tongue.

Aborted camping trips. Weekend parties missed. Christmas away from home. Lolla, who stopped inviting me for tea after a month of: "Bess has been alone all week. I can't bear listening to her whimpering as I shut the door on her face. The sound of nails scratching at the door of my thoughts." Before hanging up for the last time, Lolla saying I hid behind the dog. Good excuse not to live in the real world. True, Newfoundlanders are large enough. Strong-willed Bess could never be stopped when she set her nose on a bunny across the park. Or a cat.

I have returned to the pet store and I am staring at the same puppy, at the missing white mark on the tip of her tail, wondering whether I can bridge the longing of memory. The adorable lightness of her prancing brings me to her glimmering eye. They let me into the cage. I crouch. The puppy hops on my lap, wants someone to love her and wags her tail for as long as I remain inside the cage with her. I stroke her velvet fur. There is no one more loyal than a dog. I know it will never leave me. Never again.

"Go now," I say to the dog wagging her tail. Against her will, I push her out of the cage. "It is my time to serve," I tell her.

I lower the latch, click in my kryptonite, and lock myself from the inside.

SOPHIA'S LONGING

The day Sophia slid into bed with the other man, she had bought a pair of hand-knitted socks to fit a new-born.

II: SLOWNESS

SLOWNESS

Grandpa walks with a cane. He walks with a cane not because he feels old, not because he feels weak, but because his already, silver-haired children insist he carry one. "In the bush, alone with the grandchildren, you must use caution." Grandpa did not object, just smiled.

In the woods he trails his grandchildren.

"Deer droppings, Grandpa. Hurry, lets track them."

The children, gentle, remain determined to push him along.

"You go on, find the deer and tell me all about it. I'll sit here waiting."

The children do not wait for a second invitation. They flee in pursuit of adventure, restless after the long Grandpa delays to sniff the wild roses, and the even longer delays to engage the web-weaving spiders in conversation.

Grandpa perches on a caprock overlooking twin hoodoos on the opposite side of the valley. Inside the bubble of stillness, he dwindles to his proper size, a toad perched on a precarious mushroom landscape, and the world wide, wide as it should be. He enjoys a bird's view of the wrinkled Milk River sprawled out on its carved glacial bed. Already cottonwoods muffle the faint echo of his grandchildren, descending towards the river embankment.

It is not long before a bluebird, on a nearby juniper, delights him with its aria. The breeze which carries the soft whistling notes also perfumes him with a waft of sweetgrass. The aria crescendos. He dangles his feet over the edge of the rock. All around, yellow-bellied marmots crawl out from their dens and bask in the last rays of sunshine.

He whistles. A northern oriole puffs its orange breast and responds, whistling a crystalline, flute-like song. Grasshoppers rub their castanet wings. A pheasant, hidden among the grasses, pitches in.

He is thankful his body slowed him down after decades of rushing here, rushing there, inventing places to see, things to do, deadlines to meet. He remembers his sixties, still going strong, chasing dear life in elusive circles.

He takes a deep breath, and the wind, mysterious, lifts a White Admiral butterfly that ballets in the breeze, twirling and leaping to the tempo of the birdsong. The ground, a colourful mosaic, reveals smudges of pink and dabs of yellow, where clusters of shooting stars and patches of prickly-pear cactus flower. The sun begins to sink behind the coulee. The day is dying. The mule deer abandon the shelter of the peach-leaf willows lining the river edge and graze up the incline, unaware of his presence above.

Rock wrens fly in and out of hollow cliff nests. If he returns, if he returns as a bird, he wants to inhabit the sandstone cliffs. A ferruginous hawk glides the thermal. Or maybe not.

Time passes.

The faint murmur of the grandchildren grows, heralded by the wind.

A red-winged blackbird flies near his head, stirs the

sweet-grass fragrance. Down in the valley, the gregarious cliff-swallows graze the river water in their flight. Now, the din of voices reverberating on the cliffs announces the grandchildren's return. The marmots retreat to their rock dens. The birds hide in the saskatoon's foliage and the deer escape to the dense riverside willows.

Breathless, hair pasted to their damp foreheads, the thunder of the grandchildren approaches, closes in around him.

"Grandpa, we came so close to a doe." The youngest, bright-eyed, stretches her arms to better demonstrate how close. "But we hurried back so you wouldn't be bored, waiting here alone with nothing to do."

CLOSING ANOTHER DAY

Six o'clock, book in hand, black beret tilted over his angelic-thin hair, Senhor Ezequiel Faria stepped onto the cobblestone pathway, and climbed the cliff above the bay. He stretched his arms to the sinking sun, filling his chest with the early evening breeze.

Rain or shine, his neighbours counted on the familiar sound of Senhor Ezequiel dragging his clogs on the cobble-stone, tip-tap-tip-tap, moving in a slow deliberate pace towards the bluff. He bowed his head, a slight touch of his beret greeting whomever he passed. He met all with equal reverence. The cats that yawned on window sills, stirring from lazy afternoon naps, were reminded at his passage to ready themselves for the night prowl.

Throughout the years his neighbours never interfered with Senhor Ezequiel's daily routine. They approached their windows, out of habit, content with the familiar sight as if they were witnessing the sun closing another predictable day. "Ah ... there goes good old Senhor Ezequiel!"

The neighbours understood the inexorable tick-tock of time in Senhor Ezequiel's walk, moving one clog in front of the other, tip-tap-tip-tap.

His expected stop occurred with Lobo, Dona Branca's

german shepherd, with whom he paused and voiced a few words, inaudible to anyone else. He patted Lobo's head; a privilege not even allowed to his owner. Lobo nuzzled against Senhor Ezequiel's leg. Anyone else would have received the full blast of his bark and a flash of canine incisors as Lobo pulled on the restraining iron chain.

Senhor Ezequiel lived oblivious to the neighbourhood's reliance on his evening stroll — prompting them to draw the curtains on their day. As Senhor Ezequiel passed Clementina's fruit store, she rose from her stool, leaned against the threshold, reeled in the store's orange awning, before turning the lock on her working day. Even Dona Branca, known for her stern temperament, crocheting on the door step, bloomed in a smile at the sound of his refreshing whistling.

In the midst of the tragedies unfolding behind the privacy of laced curtains, his neighbours depended on Senhor Ezequiel for the comfort of routine. A couple suspended their argument as he walked underneath their window. Little Camila wiped old, disappointed tears, and smiled in response to his salute.

"What are you doing going up the cliff every day, Senhor Ezequiel?"

Senhor Ezequiel slowed down and smiled. "I'm going to put the sun to bed, Camila. Otherwise we would never have night and rest on this street."

Tip-tap-tip-tap. Tick-tock, tick-tock. Even if for only a moment, Senhor Ezequiel's walk pulled the neighbours out of themselves, into the passage of time.

TREED

Wait.

Yes you, power-walking through the Forest. Eyes set on the highest Peak, set on the promise of wider vistas.

Wait. Stop.

Listen to my Needles rattling a wild song. Who are you running away from? Your long, determined stride multiplies the distance between us. Me, a mere Tree, for centuries now in a gradual stroll sending my Roots over the lip of the Hill; the Hill you will reach in seconds. Roots advance at measureless speed, thin scratches on the surface of a Forest's secret.

Dandelion Seeds riding the Autumn Wind cannot overtake you as your impatient eyes glide over the undressing landscape. Imagine resting at my feet, sitting at length under the protection of my Trunk, sending Roots as one sends messages or kisses to distant loved ones. Stop! Yes you, fit and cosmopolitan, you, whom fellow joggers admire and envy. You, rushing through the Forest at dusk, after the workday, believing you can read the Trees as the standing hairs on your nape decipher the fears in your heart.

One day, centuries and centuries past, tired of hurrying, I too, arrived on this slope to enjoy the vista of Flint Lake. My body complained, a restlessness which sent Needles of discomfort into every skin pore. In time, the view of the Lake

Waters softened the discomfort. To my surprise, I could not part. I had sat long. My flesh sprouted slender Shoots into the Ground, rooting me. In previous lives I fled the slightest sign of carnal discomfort, that slight tear of skin, which revealed the pain of growing closer, deeper into other, into Earth. A matter that matters.

As I sat idle, the entire Forest arrived. The Wind delivered me the scent of Wild Lilies in bloom. The Robins nested on my Limbs, their homes balanced in the curls of my Needles. Now, the elusive Wolves and Cougars bead the hours in my shade and, at times, sleep coiled around my Trunk. At my feet, among tall Grass, rest the Sun-bleached Antlers of a Deer. The scent of Pine Needles is my own perspiration. My skin weathered, I am of the Forest. And if you would sit with me I would show you the scars on my Trunk where the Cougar sharpens her Claws to sign: Home. Or I could show you the hollow of my eye where the Red Woodpecker nests and, in Morse code, drums the news of the Land.

The aging and frayed among you recognise me. They peer upwards toward my crown, my spindly Needles, harder to grow, and even more difficult to hold onto with each passing season. Trailing behind, your old, often leaning on a Bough, stop and smell the Air, they listen to the Forest's secrets whispered in the Wind. They notice the Spiders weaving their deadly tapestries and when their fingertips touch me they sigh in acceptance. The Wind bends what remains of my Limbs, and the slow-moving trace their fingers over my wrinkled skin. I recognise the Dew in their eyes. They lay their cane next to the Sun-bleached Antlers and crawl around my feet to rest.

Ravens circle lower and lower.

THE BRIDGE

Florindo Ramos fell into the grey area between the village's fool and the village's saint. There were those, mostly women, who listened to his every word as if it were gospel; there were the others, mostly men, who laughed at every word he uttered.

After the last, never-to-be-forgotten, encounter between Florindo and Ti Marcelino, believers and sceptics alike now fled his company fearing the hand of fate and an approaching death sentence, when, in good faith, he offered to reveal the visions that crowded his mind.

The villagers remembered the time Ti Marcelino Mudo, perpetually eager to ridicule Florindo Ramos about his prophetic abilities, asked Florindo, and for his last time, about the day of his death, adding with a teasing wink, that he planned to visit the tailor on the named afternoon, to splurge on expensive silk, before drawing his last breath. "Better go out in style, don't you reckon?" He spat out his chewing tobacco in a spray of laughter.

Silent, Florindo Ramos chewed on a withered grass stem.

"Your days are numbered," he said after an uncomfortable and long pause. "On the market day of the thirteenth, you will die on the wooden bridge before reaching the crossroad to Oliveira."

The crowd dispersed in a murmur and Ti Marcelino

Mudo found himself laughing alone. He shrugged, dismissing the omen. After a day of drinking in village tavern he headed toward the bridge arguing with himself, kicking the occasional stick or crag with the misfortune of having been found in his path home.

A week later, on market day, Ti Marcelino ignored his foretold destiny. At the wooden bridge on his return home, however, Florindo Ramos' words echoed in his mind. Mortified, he stopped, glanced over his shoulder and discerned no place to turn. The food tent, already folded away, cast only the ghost of its presence in the lingering odour of grilled sardines and spilled *vinho tinto*. In the distance, the last trucks awaited the last load of unsold merchandise: cloth, skinned rabbits, plucked chickens, headless pigs, bijouterie.

Dusk.

Night would soon follow. He had lost the hours in the tavern, having raised, in toast, a few glasses more than usual. His wife and children would wait at home, potatoes steaming on the table. If Florindo's predictions would prove true he faced his last fifty paces ahead.

He stared the length of the bridge. What could possibly kill him in fifty paces? How could one stare death in the face and not recognise it? He gathered courage and dragged his feet on, slow and painful steps. Halfway across the bridge he heard the growl of an engine. Prepared, forewarned for the coward arrival of death from behind, he sprinted in a drunken zigzag course. He gained a safe ten meters of distance over death when, in his haste, he forgot the gap between the planks at the end of the bridge, tripped on his thoughts and fell head first, without mercy, toward the dusty road and a jutting crag awaiting him since the previous week when it had been last kicked by Ti Marcelino.

ROSES, LILACS, AND CHRYSANTHEMUMS

As he walked through the olive grove on an auburn summer evening, Florindo Ramos foresaw his death and, in a shiver that resembled a harvest-shaken olive tree shedding its last fruit, lost his ability to speak. He endured the ominous summer days squatting by the Rio Caima, where in silence, he watched its crystalline waters meander through the verdant valley and out of sight.

Florindo enacted the scene in his mind, knelt over his own body, motioned the closing of his eyes, followed the crowd home where they deposited his corpse, then helped them to remove his torn clothes and to bathe him, blushing for he was a modest man. Florindo's fingers traced the pools of bruises covering his skin. Deep bruises, the colour of ill ponds, lighter bruises, the colour of summer skies. Later, he sat vigil with the villagers, moved to tears by the inundation of flowers, the singing, and the feverish prayers. He joined his own funeral procession singing louder than the rest, and no one noticed. He sat next to the priest at his Seventh Day Mass and joined the congregated in sacred communion.

That summer, Florindo Ramos dug his own burial pit and slept in his grave, becoming acquainted with his flesh's final abode, searching out the most comfortable position for his eternal rest. A man of tormented sleep, he lay on his back gazing at the stars. His bones complained, heaven so far above, beyond his reach. After a month of trials, tossing and turning, he settled on his belly, the best vantage point for observing the approaching worms.

The villagers watched Florindo Ramos veiled in the morning mists at the mouth of the Rio Caima, squatting without a fishing line, mesmerized by the current. By midday, during the *sesta* and while the others rested, Florindo paced from Oliveira's crossroad to his home, then to the graveyard and the church. A daily ritual performed in earnest silence. He walked about as if he were invisible in the world, already a shadow from beyond. Some speculated that he had seen the world's apocalyptic end. Some guessed that he might have encountered a ghost. Despite their musings, no one succeeded in extricating the truth.

The day of his predestined death, and for the first time since his vision, Florindo Ramos bathed in the Rio Caima and groomed himself, parting his hair to perfection. He dressed in his black suit, knowing it would be torn to shreds. He walked through the market crowd lifting his hat, thanking people beforehand for the splendid roses, lilacs, and chrysanthemums each one would bring to his funeral. They would remember his wishes.

Before proceeding to his death, Florindo Ramos made a detour to the grave digger's house and voiced his special instructions, belly-down, no casket. Stopping next door at the church, he pointed out to Padre Lucas the scriptures he wished read at his funeral: "Of those who lie sleeping in the dust of the earth many will awake," from the Book of Daniel, and, "It is good and holy to think of the dead rising again," from the Maccabees.

By the time he finished his errands and voiced his private goodbyes, hundreds of the villagers trailed Florindo Ramos like a procession. They were curious. How could one confront death on such a sunny and glorious day? Not a hint of a breeze to topple a tree onto him (Cipriano Bispo's fate years before), not a thunder cloud in sight to fulminate him like Rossandra Ferreira. After completing a perfect circle around the village wall, Florindo stopped. His back to the crowd, he faced the hollow darkness of the village portal. The portal funnelled a marble glow from the cemetery in the distance. He looked up for the omen. Out of the cloudless blue sky a jet plane crossed overhead. A roar louder than thunder shook the ground and a white apocalyptic line slashed through the air, convincing the religious-minded that Florindo Ramos had predicted the end of the world. In panic, the herd of villagers stampeded towards the protective walls trampling everything in their path.

Later, and on the rare occasion that the thunderous roar returned to slash the white apocalyptic line in their haunted sky, the villagers would drop their scythes, hammers or kettles and hurry to Florindo's headstone to huddle in prayer, freshening his grave with roses, lilacs, and chrysanthemums. Florindo Ramos, they believed, averted the end of the world by offering his life to God. A saintly death, so that their lives could be spared. The villagers remembered Florindo's funeral scriptures and prayed by his graveside, waiting for the day when he would awaken and return to free their troubled consciences.

Florindo Ramos, awakening from his eternal rest, moved to tears by the inundation of flowers, would smell each flower and join his people in their feverish hymns, singing louder than anyone else, yet no one ever noticed.

Years passed. The villagers returned with less and less frequency until his memory rested forgotten. Florindo Ramos, tired of rising up to the silence and neglect of his grave, at last succumbed to his end.

THE WEEKEND

Constant buzz of traffic, punctuated by accelerating motorbikes, invades Lino's bedroom. A slight heaviness weighs in his head. The almost deaf neighbour in the flat below blasts his TV and Lino lies in bed listening to the freshly displayed tragedies of the day. He enjoys a lethargic waking, accustoms his eyes to the penumbra in the room. After a couple of hours staring at the ceiling, when the discomfort of complacency stirs his bones and the sound of a sizzling frying pan on a cooking show tempts his grumbling stomach, he jumps to his feet.

In the dimness, before finding the fridge, Lino collides with a chair and bumps his head on a cupboard door. He scoops out a bowl of ice cream for breakfast and turns on his own TV for company. Music videos. He ensures that it is turned up louder than the neighbour's.

Lino fears opening the roman blinds to another grey depressing day, to the sad city with its exhaust-stained buildings and perpetual curse of a drizzle. After he licks his ice-cream bowl and spoon with meticulous care, Lino rolls up the blinds. A wave of light inundates the room. Heat tingles his skin. Despite his closed eyes, an idea illuminates his mind. He should plan something for such a beautiful and inviting day. He will spend the day at the beach. It is always pleasant by the sea. Gulls and surf. Nothing strenuous. Besides, he enjoys people-watching. But he will wait until four o'clock. The public announcements on TV repeat warnings not to expose fair skin during mid-day hours to harmful rays from the depleted ozone layer. A deadly affair, that tragedy with the ozone layer. Lino grabs a day pack and dawdles around the house stuffing in a towel, comics — not having patience for the endless monotony of words — a 30 SPF sun protector, a bottle of water, a toenail clipper. Lino counts an hour to kill. The phone rings. Phones insist in interrupting the normal unfolding of his day. He enters the shower to drown the irritating sound.

It is four o'clock and the phone has stopped ringing. He parts his wet hair in the middle and remembers he waited all week for an hour-long TV special on the Beatles. Lino lies on the couch, watches the show. The show finishes. He eats a hot dog and notices the rush hour traffic pandemonium rattling the beer bottle collection along the living room walls. He cannot risk driving now. He recalls the horrible accidents on city streets at peak traffic. He will wait a couple more hours. There will be less confusion at the beach by then, the sun inoffensive and dimming. He can count in years the time since he has seen a sunset. Lino searches for his video camera in the *new projects* box. He finds it buried under a snorkel and fins, a karaoke mike and a kite. A flash of excitement travels up his spine. What better day could he find to initiate his long-awaited home-video hobby? Placing the camera in the beach sack, he removes the tube of sunscreen. A little sun at the end of the day will replenish his vitamin D requirement. He will save on supplements.

Lino changes the TV channel and checks on the traffic reports. A bad accident west of the beach boulevard and traffic jams clog access to the area. Announcers recommend driving on alternate routes.

Lino calculates that by the time the area clears up, the forty-five minute drive will bring him to his destination after sunset. Danger lurks in the city after sunset and he abhors the idea of being caught outside in the dark. It invites trouble or hideous crimes.

Lino snaps open a beer, and absentmindedly follows an "All You Need is Love" TV contest. A dull ache spreads in his chest, hard to pinpoint the epicentre. He makes an appointment with his doctor through her answering machine. Damn, all he needs now is to fall sick at the end of his holidays. He worries. Monday, the office expects him back at work. The dull ache continues.

Lino phones for two All-Meats pizzas, a shrimp Caesar salad, Chicago fries and onion rings, black forest cake, and an apple pie. He orders both a Coke and a Pepsi, still uncertain which he likes best. The movie channel features two great classics — *Grease* and *Saturday Night Fever*.

Lino sinks down into his love-seat and settles in.

ZEN AND THE
ART OF LAUNDRY

I confess that my repulsion prevented me from being close to Todd in the four years we shared a room in college. I don't think Todd understood the meaning of the word laundry. It was not part of his vocabulary, not part of his DNA as it is for the rest of us.

Todd piled his clothes on the dusty wooden floor by our bedroom bay window. The sun hung around that banished geography of the room for the better side of the day. Todd knew then something I didn't.

In fairness I must say Todd never clung to the same outfit longer than a week. That way he demonstrated common sense. A guy with integrity, Todd stood by his principles and followed his own rules to the comma and the full stop. That meant the last worn outfit would land faithfully on top of the growing pile of worn clothes. No exceptions; even if they were his favourite brown suede trousers and café au lait polo shirt. Café au lait represented as festive a colour as he ever displayed. "Autumn colours don't show the dirt," he once mentioned in passing.

"Why not use a basket?" I suggested.

"Clothes, like us, require space to vent their stinking frustrations and spread their sleeves."

It might be relevant to mention Todd majored in philosophy with a double minor in ethics and religious studies, and that his laundry cycle lasted one month before each piece of clothing's turn came up. Needless to say Todd did not indulge in frivolous temptations. Trousers and shirts mated for life in his universe of affections. The essence of his thoughtful demeanour could be captured by the slow movement of his laundry cycle. For most of us forty-five minutes sufficed for a rapid wash, while his laundry cycle followed the rhythms of nature: the return of the full moon.

That pile of clothes became Todd's living sculpture; a mound of clothes catching their breath, aging before the sun, only to return to the streets in the full body of its vintage. The process respected the ancient footsteps of making a treasured wheel of aged cheddar and proved equally as stimulating to the olfactory glands.

I understand now it takes commitment to be green, it takes vision to save the planet. One must step beyond the anti-septic vision of the lifeless and change the tide on our understanding of cleanness.

"Let's us not be neurotic about germs, germs are us. Besides, the sun is our best disinfectant," Todd shouted, his arms flailing as he attempted to stand his moral ground against his mother during her first surprise visit to our quarters. According to Todd's philosophy he found no noble reason to waste water on cloth either. He referred his mother and the rest of his critics to the footnotes of history on Tibetan and Scottish cultures.

After that first visit, Todd's mother established a bi-annual pilgrimage across the continent at which time the pile would momentarily vanish, returning scented and folded in his mother's arms. Todd did not have a good relationship with his mother.

Except for those few days of deep depression following his mother's visit as he carried the apocalyptical end of the world on his shoulders while pacing the room under a cloud of enforced sterilization, Todd's clothes or himself never smelled so artificial. Aside from this, on all other days, inside out, nothing to mask, he stank all around. No fake scents to trigger a headache. No masking. No icing on the shit. True and through.

The scientist on the radio urges me to apply radical changes to my lifestyle if I were serious about saving the planet, changes beyond the token *green this and green that*, the effortless options of irrelevant effect. I realize Todd lived ahead of his time and that is the reason he is not the Minister of fake smells who gives me a headache during his budget speech while standing across the parliament bench and radiating his overpowering and artificial sweetness.

I have far more respect for Todd now. It takes time to understand people who stand up for something.

ALLEVIATIONS

The dull hum of patients seeps through the wall, the solemn whisper people adopt in a hospital waiting room. A seriousness only matched in places of devotion. The sound of shuffling feet intensifies as the day progresses. He coughs, stares at an enlarged reprint of Monet's *Water Lilies*, and imagines Spring spreading inside the sterile building, contaminating the walls with colour.

He strolls to the door and with the curl of his finger signals the next patient to enter. This is one of the days he must be diligent and patient, he thinks, as he recognises the man shuffling his feet toward the door. The man hesitates before stepping in the office, patting the soiled patch over his eye with resignation.

"Didn't I tell you to change the gauze after a week?"

The man mumbles, shrugs one shoulder, pushes his will over the threshold of the door, squints at the painting, before he finds the hardwood chair missing a slat.

"I did. But I hurt myself again."

The blackened patch, likely from a mindless hand rubbing, resembles a bruise.

"You can't expect miracles if you don't do what you are told." He is annoyed. Not annoyed from repeating the same advice to different people, annoyed at repeating the same advice to the same people.

He pretends not to hear the patient's question until the patient asks him again.

"No, my cough is not improving. But we are not here to cure my cough, are we?" he says and pulls his chair closer. "Now let's get to the business of removing this patch."

A firm believer that education held the secret to changing behaviour, he attempted a myriad of strategies to change patients' habits. Never with success.

"Let's see what's growing under there."

He removes the patch. The eye, swollen, bloodshot, drowns in scarlet. He sighs, frustrated. Every few months he removes splinters from this patient's eyes. The man, a sculptor, repeats that he is sorry, he forgets to wear goggles when chiselling. He blames the tools, he blames the times. The tools more powerful, the stone weaker. God help him, but he only remembers to look for his goggles after a splinter has already flown in. "God damn, it hurts," the man tells him.

"Will you wear goggles or will you walk in here blind one day?"

In time, his patients repent, always too late. He has heard the range of excuses. Makes them crazy to have something covering their eyes. They see better the plain way.

He wonders what he should say to the patient to change his mind. He picks up tweezers and decides not to use anaesthetic this time. Perhaps the memory of pain will be a better reminder than innocuous words. Indeed, the body carries vivid memories of pain before it remembers a word. He coughs, spits blood into the enamel spittoon at his feet.

The tweezers bite the marble chip and the patient moans. His chest hurts. It's chronic now.

"I won't see you next time if you come with another splinter!" He says it without conviction, knowing he will continue to respond to his patients' suffering. Alleviating pain, even the needless, stupid suffering of people hopeless to change is a pleasure to him. He squeezes out two drops of disinfectant, followed by five drops of an antibiotic and dresses the patient's eye.

With a half-annoyed face, he writes down a quick prescription and waves the man away.

"See you back here in a month, then."

He waits for the door to close and tilts back and forth in his chair. The chair squeaks its annoying countdown with each motion. He lights another cigarette before the next appointment and strolls to an enlarged poster of the human iris. The dark background of the cosmos highlights the star-like colours of the iris. It glows and relaxes him. Small consolation for sitting in a windowless cubicle from sunrise to sunset.

THE MOVING MOUNTAIN

The daisies on the roadside vanished before his eyes, even before he could consider their colour or imagine their scent.

Tenzin peered from the back seat of the car, observed his serene master riding in the front passenger seat. The master's hands rested on his lap, thumbs touched. Tenzin noted his own knuckles, white, gripping the door handle. The car roared around a dirt curve on the mountain pass, disappeared in the dust. In silence, Tenzin repeated a mantra of impermanence, his eyes planted on the void. Goats grazed below the road, tucked in the ravine, and interrupted their hunger to gaze upward at the car, their bells muffled by the roaring metal tiger echoing against the rocky escarpment. The goats stood camouflaged as black and white clouds on the green slopes.

"Monks live at one with the divine and fear nothing, right?" The young driver grinned.

"It is very kind of you to offer us a ride." Tenzin's master thanked the driver with a slight tilt of his head.

Dust entered the driver's window, stung Tenzin's eyes. The car spun around a curve, its rear end a slithering dragon.

Be in the moment. Tenzin recalled his master's words.

The moment highlighted the demon of fear. Tenzin, certain he rode his last journey, thanked the sunshine, the flowers, even the present unsettling ride to an uncertain destination. He prepared himself.

The driver honked, and startled pedestrians squeezed against the carved out trail on the hill. The driver slapped the steering wheel and laughed with abandon. "People frighten for nothing!" Unpreoccupied with the road, he stared at Tenzin's master. "Horror movies are my favourite. What are yours?"

"I don't watch movies. I have nightmares."

"You should watch movies," the young man said in a devout tone. "Life- changing," he added after a measured thought. "They wake you up. And that's like being enlightened, right?"

The young driver tailed a truck filled with pigs and battered the horn. The animals squealed, helpless, and struggled to escape crowded quarters. With his sleeve, Tenzin wiped beads of fear collecting on his corrugated brow. The young driver overtook the truck on the approaching curve. Tenzin's eyes widened as a donkey cart trotted toward them. The truck driver slammed the brakes, veered into the ditch. The car squeezed through the moving keyhole of a miracle.

"There's always someone else more afraid than you," the driver whispered, relieved.

Tenzin brought his short and anxious breath back into his body, his heart. The tightness in his chest eased. He stared through the fright in his eyes, wiped the dust-filled window with his sleeve and stared with concern past the clear glass.

Lives hurried past through the window view. Around a bend and behind a shrub, two children hurried a kiss. The baskets on their heads touched in view of their parents who walked behind pulling carts loaded with vegetables. The parents smiled. A burial procession exited a stone house, blended in against the mountainside. Mothers carried children tied to kerchiefs on their backs.

The driver accelerated around another curve. The wheels caught gravel. The car slid sideways, off the road and into the emptiness of the ravine. The driver tightened his fists on the steering wheel. His rigid body pressed the brakes. His face contorted in fear. A scream filled the car. Quiet, Tenzin and his master smiled, palm touching palm and over their heart, as they stared at the beautiful granite approaching.

TIME IN SEARCH OF A BODY

A blur of bodies swept to and fro, blue or white depending on their role, a few angelic, others not. He waited, on a stretcher, blue tag on a wrist, tucked along the wall of the corridor.

The woman, in white, asked his name again, asked his birth date, asked the nature of his impending surgery. The metal rattle of his stretcher's bones announced unexpected motion as she wheeled him through a zigzag of corridors.

In the operating room, the silence weighed on the slow motion of instruments circulated from hand to hand. The doors closed. The cold sparseness and the clinking metals reminded him of torture chambers on another continent. Another woman in blue introduced herself and again asked for a history of allergies. Of the anaesthetic, she explained the sensation to arrive in his throat before he would disappear under the veil of induced sleep. He sensed the split second of timelessness approaching, swift as a scalpel.

Time searched for memory. Time searched for a body where to dwell and recognize itself. Time, homeless above the body in the operating room. No one warned him surgeons had planned to fish him out of his life stream to give him more time and perhaps temporarily save him. They had spoken of a mere restful sleep. They lied. Across many longitudes his father and mother sat by a phone, wringing hands. His wife with two young children, only a thin wall away, understood the gravity of the lie and paced the corridor of sterile air under the weight of a frown.

The surgeons resuscitated him, although no one but he believed him dead for those few hours under the silence of memory, lullabied by the music of metal instruments clanking, digging and sawing on his bony body. In the arms of death he was certain he had been.

His body opened one eye, for an instant, then a minute, confused about his whereabouts. The woman in white next to him again asked his name. He had returned from a journey, a journey without memory. A journey without a dream. Was this his body? His eyes swirled with the drunkenness of a bottle spinning in a current. Time had returned in the stalled task of a thought and the unfocused outline of a perhaps. Perhaps that was his name slipping off his lips, and perhaps not. He clung to the smooth, icy metal of the stretcher's bar until the woman in white permitted his wife next to him. Time travelled with snail legs into his eyes and through the steep veins of his body. In genuine sleep, he never abandoned his body. He carried his body into his dreams, dressed it in other sizes and contours, in other faces and colours. Not this time after leaving the operating room. The weight of time pressed on his words and the words stumbled out inarticulate, "Where am I?"

Within one year, he had become a regular in this timeless room. His hair turned white. He lost time.

He found a hand to hold. Skin provided the necessary sticky properties to trap time. At first, any hand would serve. Later, awake and relaxed, only particular hands would hold time. In the grasp of an unacquainted hand, his time slipped through their skin pores and he continued his free-fall into his nightmare of loneliness which was in reality the nightmare of separation from everything, including his body. Even later, a month later, at times, he would want someone at his bedside or in his vicinity. "The moment white coats inhabit my dreams, I am alone. I have died," he whispered to his wife. His wife squeezed his hand. She recognized the texture of his words.

On that first pale hand, he anchored himself from the void, described as pain without a memory of the pain. A ghost pain. A disembodied pain. His body awoke quartered up, sliced, wounded, bloodied, scared and scarred with a paragraph of its history missing; disoriented, without having witnessed the deleterious act, without having named the hand that inflicted the pain. Eyes blindfolded by the haze of anaesthetic, despite the crescent awakening pain, arriving now from another time and place as though late for an injury. That strange body he now inhabited did not know where to catalogue the present. The surgery mimicked the gestures of any barbaric invasion through history, a forced resettlement of the body. The body lingered, a blind witness, without a story or a thread to weave meaning into its fabric. "Peace is to leave the flesh alone to make amends with its memories," he whispered to his wife who this time clung to his hand and hid her apprehension behind a smile of reassurance.

The woman in white propped him up at his request. He lifted his hand to trace the new scars. Scars imprinted on the music score of his skin, marked interruptions and interventions; a collection of inerasable notations that would never leave him or be out of print. Blood thumped, the globules tumbled around in his veins; sweepers cleaning, maintaining the flow, the living, while his life carried on inside a Leonard Cohen song, sprinkled with blank notes and static.

His mind awoke anxious. No one had warned his body that anxiousness was the poisoning residue of anaesthesia — general or nine to five. Forced to sleep without a dream, the memory had fallen off synch with the body; a gap opened in the terrain, interrupted his continuous narrative; time again lost, and behind. The door to the beginning of madness had creaked slightly open; the condition palpable in the compressing of his chest; an oppression that he could not point his finger at, a weight he could not lift with the push of his hand.

THE READING

The poet approached the stage. His languid shadow moved ahead of him, projected onto the coal-tainted side-wall—the enormity of the shadow prompted the poet to stop, undecided on whether to step into it and be swallowed or continue to stalk it as a predator.

At the rim of the stage, the poet scrutinised the emcee at the microphone. He sent him a nod. The emcee blinked, read a not-so-humble biographical note, written by the poet himself. The poet scanned the audience buried in the dark. Background conversations subsided. Verbal driftwood from downstairs travelled up the swirling staircase, washed in upon the audience's ears. Pressed against the last shore of tables, people stood and waited.

In one hand, he carried his book, in the other, a pint of beer. With the awkwardness of the non-athletic whose centre of gravity had long slipped to the far edge of its extended belly, the poet swung one foot onto the stunted stage. A rocking motion propelled him forward and a touch upward. An expressive grunt preceded his entrance in the spotlight. The beer in his hand spilled a few drops. He stopped to evaluate the marks on the floor and mourn the loss.

The poet held onto the mug, set the book on the tall

loudspeaker next to the microphone. He sipped the beer, squinted, inspecting the audience. He smiled to himself. With the free hand, he removed his thick eyeglasses, fogged the lenses with his breath, before rubbing them in circular motions on his red shirt. His black vest revealed an unidentifiable palette of old meals and drinks.

Intent on soaking up the sweat collecting on his brow, the poet slid his forearm across his forehead and froze in a rehearsed pose. He cleared his throat and brought his mouth to the microphone. The crackle of nacho chips and clinking of glasses halted. Expectant, the audience watched. Their adrenaline filled the air. The abrupt silence dropped the temperature in the room. On stage, the theatre of his mind unfolded. The poet dragged the rake of his fingers through his hair, stopped in surprise, noticing his talisman missing. He forced another grin, raked the stub of his fingers over his head in repetitive motions, searched for the hat lying forgotten on the bar counter. Thinning, oily hair pasted his forehead. He pressed his forearm to his forehead, soaked the spills of sweat.

The audience stirred. In the absence of words, the weight of silence pressed. The poet's slow gestures scratched the silence and revealed what the audience was not prepared to receive: unmediated wounds. Returning his slipping eyeglasses to the bridge of his veined nose, the poet retrieved his book from the loudspeaker and, still holding onto the pint, opened the book to what appeared a random page. Hello, he voiced at last. His gaze found refuge on the page. Half-muttered words explained his life as a poet and the birth of that particular poem. Slurred words could not negotiate the dark and congested path to the end of the room where whispers mushroomed. The audience leaned forward, faces hovered above the drinks. The poet's white stubble glimmered in the spotlight, a sheen that brightened his plump and cratered face.

The poet stretched the book away from his face, as far as his short arms would permit; he took another sip of the beer and began his poem. One person laughed aloud, giggles erupted for the comical stanza about drunkards. Surprised, the poet stopped, raised his eyes and at last met the audience. Delighted, he nodded, saying, *good, good.* When he realized he had lost his last word, frantic, he searched the page while his sequence of hmmms, grunts and ahhhs grated the audience.

Ten more poems followed. After each successive poem the desperate applause crescendoed. The poet's chest inhaled more of the stale air in the room and inflated in accordance. After his twelfth poem, he informed the audience he would present his last. The audience, now adrift, conversing, showered the poet with applause. Encouraged, basking in the ovation, the poet read an additional last poem. One more sip of the caramel-coloured liquid remained in the pint. When the poet pulled a cigarette from his breast pocket, his decorative red handkerchief fell without his notice, pooled at his feet mimicking a fresh blood stain. Without lighting his cigarette, he slid it to the side of his lip where it hung in precarious balance. He considered lighting the smoke, reasoning that, despite the law, no one would dare stop him from puffing on stage. The act would confirm a poet's outlaw status in any stage, any century. With dismay, he realised he'd forgotten the lighter underneath his hat at the bar counter.

After his fourteenth poem, an indiscernible mumble with the unlit cigarette dangling from a corner of the mouth, the audience exploded into applause once again. When the applause did not subside, the poet, nevertheless, attempted the fifteenth poem. Undeterred, the clapping reached a climax drowning out the poet's words. The poet beamed, grinned. The cigarette dropped. His reddened face shone, a setting sun on stage. Shifting from foot to foot, giddy, the poet took another gulp of the beer in his hand, tilting his head back. The wetness of beer did not follow the ecstasy of words. Disappointed, the poet fastened his gaze to the inside of the empty pint. The applause continued. He looked at the audience, at this book and at the pint. He pondered this equation in reverse order, paused, raised the hand holding the book and, saluting the audience, touched the book to his forehead before he proceeded to the side of the stage. The roar of applause intensified. The poet strolled to the rear of the bar, his shadow following him this time. He nodded and beamed at the patrons downing their drinks, eyes averted, before he disappeared in the hollow of his shadow and the dark tide of undefined bodies.

THE FACE

A rosy glow of health, he says.
A burn, she says.
Sunset, he says.
Inferno, she says.

His cheerful grin raises the gamble.

A waterfront face of notches, blotches of glowing skin, of blue broken vessels, frames the raised Tequila Sunrise twirling in his hand. Outside, on the beach, the sun drowns, sinking into immense liquid, unable to swim. A string of inaudible words floats in the air before he loses his balance and, unannounced, darkness surrounds him. The night has fallen, flattening the ocean.

The red tequila liquid glows against the white kitchen tiles and the splintered glass has risen in a thousand glimmering stars. She is shattered, stares at his face. One eye follows the strings of blood, currents, winds, mapping his skin and her gaze pauses around his temple. She kneels. The strings of blood intertwine to braid a web-like trap. Her other eye notices the faint naiveté of his smile, a fluttering butterfly in a garden of innocence.

The scarlet dye stains the once immaculate tile. His

nose throbs, swells, a brave nose, a foolish nose ahead of himself, an unreliable rudder in the course of life, not smelling danger, not even today when it cracked against the implacable cold floor. He is broken, a rudderless vessel, defenceless in the face of mundane winds whirling him in aimless, vicious circles.

She screams as both eyes converge. She assembles the fragmented picture. The fluttering wings of his smile will brush against the tightening web, and life will cease, trapped in this knot of broken vessels.

III: BENEATH OUR BEDS

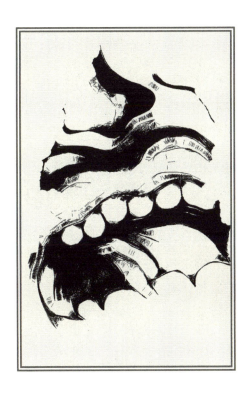

THE MIDWIFE OF TORMENT

Florindo Ramos fell, head first, through the outhouse hole in the public gardens. After his mother heard the screams and rushed to fish him out, she immediately hosed him down in the public courtyard and washed the obvious. At home, she boiled a cauldron of water for a good scrub and bathed him in rose petals, washing the folds of his ears with the hem of her skirt. Nonetheless, Florindo Ramos never believed he would be clean again.

At night, tossing between lavender-scented sheets, unable to shake the curse of the outhouse stench that haunted his sleep, Florindo Ramos would regurgitate his evening meal. By day, he carried handkerchiefs in every pocket, which he moistened with spittle to rub his face clean. From continuous scrubbing, sores developed and, repulsed by his festering face, little by little, people began to avoid him. In Florindo's eyes, this proved that he remained unclean.

Felismina, the village *curandeira*, a woman accustomed to probing the depths of the psyche, a midwife of torment, heard about Florindo's condition. She believed him. "If the boy says he stinks, he stinks. Who are we? Do we wear his skin, smell his nightmares?"

Florindo Ramos sought her intercession in the matter.

After consulting her wrinkled manuals, brushing the dust off her skirt, Felismina declared: "I dug up one antidote, boy. Only one. But, for it to work you must be willing to look the nightmare in the face."

Florindo shuddered, scrubbed his face with the handkerchief in his hand.

"Unless you want to live with things as they are ...," Felismina said, closing her manual. A cloud of dust rose in the air.

Florindo's hands trembled and his eyes shone white with fear, but before the end of the day he nodded in assent.

"I can't promise it will work without the help of the others," Felismina concluded.

When Felismina announced her plan, half the people stomped away complaining, "Why in heavens can't we use the water from our clean mountain spring?"

"We need to fight alike with alike," Felismina answered. "It's everyone's excrement we're discussing." In truth no one could deny using the public outhouse at one time or another. "Therefore," she insisted, "it's our refuse at the bottom of the outhouse. All of us are implicated in Florindo's torment."

Despite efforts to avoid Florindo, people encountered him queuing at the bakery or the butcher, kneeling beside them in church, where mindless he picked at his scabs, the yellow and red ooze trickling down his face. They could not avert their eyes, and soon, their thoughts. In time people became convinced that Florindo's problem was everyone's problem and no one would have peace of mind until Florindo regained his own. Some resisted, more reluctant to help than others. Those of religious inclination consulted first the priest, then the Bible and found no literal objections to the concoction. In the end, everyone committed to help Florindo prepare the potion which would wash his torment away.

With the approach of the full moon, the village people gathered the ingredients, filling the fountain with the intimate recipe.

At midnight, on the full moon, with steam rising from the magic concoction, a procession — from toddlers in mothers' arms to elders leaning on stronger shoulders — congregated around the fountain, night potties in hand. One by one, they stepped out of their shoes, and into the depths of the boy's nightmare, taking turns bathing Florindo Ramos, from his toes to the folds of his ears.

SONIA'S CONSCIOUS BELIEF IN THE UNCONSCIOUS

Sonia consciously believed in the unconscious, believed in everything that slipped between her fingers in grains of sand. Sand in cogs. Sand in teeth, grinding life to a halt. She believed dreams, the blessed messages from the stars — warnings, omens, insights from another world, another language. Sonia studied her dreams as others studied the skies and watched the clouds to predict the approaching changes of weather. Dreams generated winds inside her life — bad and good — shaping her future. When her mother shook her head in disbelief, Sonia reminded her of the wind, that invisible hand shaping landscape into Wonderlands and Badlands. Wind shuttled the black clouds away, erased the dreams degenerating into nightmares.

Before sleep, faithful, Sonia recited a mantra to encourage her memory to remember her dreams the following morning. It will work magic, her self-help book had guaranteed. *As daylight returns, you will awake in steps, hold your body motionless, not to startle the dream away, that quiet innocent bird ready to flee at the slightest disturbance. Your dream journal, by your bedside, open on a vacant page, will be prepared to be inhabited by memory.*

As night descended, Sonia entered a profound sleep. She dreamed, searched in vain, frantic, searched for anything and everything, not knowing what or why. A desperate quest for a thing she forgot, and which the world counted on, depended upon. Yet Sonia forgot, unable to comprehend, why pain, love, destruction, art, joy, dying, opening up?

In the dream, a young artist tore at his hair and sunk his nails into the palms of his skin, as frustrated, locked-out journalists and photographers scurried away from his first exhibition, from his promising future, and hurried to the next story vying for attention. A patron, upset by the gallery closure, confronted with a sudden emptiness in his planned life, crossed, absentminded, the railway tracks. A commuter train, on time, released him from schedules. Sonia dreamed that another patron, finding herself freed from a final art assignment by the gallery closure, strolled toward the river where she sat next to a stranger, soon to be her husband. She warned him that it was not a smart idea, in winter, to feed wild geese bread. Otherwise birds will never leave. The two fell in love.

Sonia woke up disturbed. A long, deep breath lifted the dust already settling over her memory. Serene, she reconstructed the dream, remembered details, the colour of clothing, the jewellery, if any. Her Jungian therapist, once a week, helped her unravel the puzzle of the unconscious, dissected her soul, word by word. The therapist insisted that the oneiric details contained the answers to all questions, they were key to the door of the unconscious. Methodical and meticulous, she wrote thirteen pages of details on the colour of the commuter train, the garments and jewellery people wore, before realising she was late for her first day on the job at the art gallery.

GRACE

Selina glides into the room. She waves gladioli in her hand and proceeds to the radio lamenting, "Oh ... dreadful silence! Let's bring a breath of life in here." Slow, Grace enters behind her.

It's the stale urine, the disinfectant, the ammonia, that sicken me. They insist I was already unwell before they admitted me, and supposedly that's a valid reason for confining me to this living graveyard where everything reeks of bleach, and glares institutional white. Selina will chatter above the radio and Grace, silent, will query my eyes and rub my feet. I will not feel her touch. We understand.

Selina tucks another photo of another grandchild around the perimeter of the wall mirror. A distant blur of reflections in the chain of memory, impossible for me to recognise now. My own enlarged picture, in the centre, bare-chested, reeling in a 200-pounder halibut is whom Selina speaks to, a reminder of vigour in life past.

The open door attracts bodies. They drift into the room and, absent, stare at the crucifix on the wall and at the world seeping through the window. Their eyes seem to ask the crucifix, that minuscule steel crossbar imprisoning them with religious fervour to this world, how much longer?

Selina hushes the bodies away and locks the door. It's then she reads aloud the prayer hanging on the wall above my head: "Lord, help me to remember that nothing will happen to me today that you and I together cannot handle." She sighs and dusts the plastic violets tucked among the photographs, growing out of the barren whiteness of the wall.

As usual, Selina leaves early to pick up her children from school. It's then that Grace silences the radio with a gleeful stab of her finger and wheels my bed to the window where the sun will caress my lips. She smiles. I see the green in the land, the blue in the sky and she wipes away my tears. Grace slides open the glass window and a breeze brings a robin to the ledge. The robin sings to me. Grace holds my hand and removes the pillow from under my head. I hope she catches the smile in my eyes. I'm saying yes, yes, and hope she remembers nothing will happen to me and her that together we cannot handle. Grace places the pillow on my face and presses. Faint, at first, my body stirs, foolish muscles. She presses with her body's weight. I see rainbows. My flesh resists in a convulsive shudder. My mouth gasps for a thread of air. Her pressure eases. Grace lifts the pillow and stares me in the eyes. I beg the only way I have left to beg. She understands.

This time Grace kisses me good-bye.

NO COBWEBS IN HEAVEN

At the age of twelve, freshly arrived at the Order of the Sisters of Immaculate Conception, Benedita had never entered an elevator. Her entire life of thirteen miserable cold winters, clinging to a rosary and kissing the rosy paper-thin cheeks of The Lady, had kept her in the dark of an isolated outport town until a first miraculous intercession by a travelling Bishop touched her life and the Sisters accepted her into the Order.

As a novice without rank, every day she earned her keep by scrubbing the three rising cloister levels and the elevator. On her first day she began at ground level, closer to earth, mimicking her life's plight. In time, she believed, the ticking hours, the increased beads of sweat and rosary prayers, the bruised knees, would earn her heavenly ascent beyond the last floor.

Benedita never questioned the hour after hour, day after day of cleaning expected of her. It seemed a reasonable, logical prospect under any plain roof that also sought order to their affairs, and most befitting of a convent's purity. In this mundane light, excessive cleaning, much like excessive praying, could never be deemed excessive. However, as with the mysteries of the divine workings of the world, the mysteries of the workings in the House of God appeared equally remarkable and she accepted the inexplicable with the innocent smile that had earned her future in this cloister.

At the end of each long, blue tiled corridor, where the spiral of stone stairs met each cloister, the elevator door poised in silent meditation and awaited its rare daily opening by hands closer to God than her own. Only the three oldest Sisters received permission to ascend the skies, travelling that much closer to the Divine after nearly a lifetime of devotion. Benedita ensured her scrubbing timing positioned her within a glimpse of that promising and opening door of heaven. As if the uplifting part of the miracle were not sufficient in itself, she blessed herself. Soon after, the Sisters' disembodied voices would also emerge, ricocheting from the granite walls of the cloisters above. Such glorious hymns of joy echoed the sanctity of the word among the higher spirits. This mundane experience offered credence to the possibility of resuscitation and the apparent effortless lifting of the spirit above any weight and on any body; even young Sister Emilia who hauled around a spirit at least four times as voluminous as Benedita's. Benedita had been concerned for this Sister's feasible ascension to heaven until the moment, last week, the elevator proved anything possible. Her ascension, and yet to arrive return, concluded the first of many mysteries yet to unveil in this convent. With the patience of the faithful, the novice nun continued scrubbing each floor on hands and knees, each time puzzling as the elevator floor appeared much cleaner on the second, and then again, the third floor. She determined that the younger Sisters living on the first floor were significantly messier.

Of the added cobweb always to be found inside the elevator's first floor and never on the two higher floors was a mystery she kept to herself, a personal confirmation there were no cobwebs in Heaven. This indeed substantiated her understanding that the closer one became to God the more immaculate the world became.

Despite the arduous tasks and heavy lifting demanded of her, and as her belly inexplicably continued to swell, Benedita worried whether she might become as large as Sister Emilia had been. To her astonishment a time did arrive when she too could no longer bend to scrub the floors. With this development also arrived her occasion to enter the elevator. The required vow of silence to join this Sisterhood no longer appeared without reason amid the hellish pains testing her vows. Sterner than ever, the older Sisters shepherded Benedita through the door of the elevator, their sombre and heavy disposition incapable of erasing the grin of elation in Benedita's face. This journey of suffering appeared to have arrived as a blessing to the devoted believer she was, and now feeling finally ripe for her journey of ascension, she radiated purity, eager to experience God that much closer.

ZÉ BAREFOOT

Not your run-of-the-mill boy, Zé Barefoot raced through corn fields alongside any other child in the village, with one distinction, he refused the skin of his feet to be separate from the earth. He relished feeling the grass tickling the underbelly of his toes and sought the coolness of the ground after a rainfall. No other child dared race him up to the crown of a tree after seeing his toes cling to the bark with the grip of a cat. In no time, he reached the swaying canopy of a cherry tree where the fruit glowed the ripest, and he sat nibbling on the fruit even before others had reached the first branch, their soles slipping on the smooth bark.

It is said his mother gave birth to Zé Barefoot in the thick of a corn field where he already dropped to the ground on bare feet and grinned at the world. All through his childhood his cries could only be soothed the moment his mother laid him on the soil of the land.

No tale or threat would convince Zé Barefoot to set foot inside a boat despite his never-met-father having been a non-returning sailor with the cod fleet to Newfoundland. Unlike his father, and perhaps because of his father, nothing would convince Zé Barefoot to leave the green grass of the valley. When his feet burrowed beneath the dirt of the fields, and he stood among stalks of corn listening to the call of the blackbird, one would almost believe him to grow out of the ground and bear fruit. No smile more radiant than Zé's could be found in the valley, not even the sun's.

The day Zé Barefoot woke up feverish and delirious, complaining the earth spun and vanished from beneath his feet, and that he fell, fell without end into a hole, his mother wanted to sit him in the church pews where he would be under the watchful eyes of every known saviour. However, the boy insisted on lying in the field, settled among the cornstalks, staring at the void of stars above, listening to the song of the wind playing harp on the corn's foliage. He refused the stethoscope of the village doctor near him, he refused the priestly prayers and holy waters, or the pelt of a rabbit stewed in bull's piss known as the last resort of the *curandeira* to spew out any malefaction hiding in the deepest nook of any body.

Only after his last shudder as Zé clung to a tuft of grass and the stem of a corn plant, did the doctor discover a hole concealed beneath the inscrutable layer of dirt on the sole of his foot. This festering hole of infection was home to maggots and their eggs, likely the result of having stepped on the sharp protrusion of a harvested cornstalk. The doctor also found stars and planets and black holes where he had imagined, Zé, in his delirium, had dove into from the height of his head. That would also explain the boy's complaining dizziness of late. He wondered what other undiscovered treasures remained inside the boy's well-worn but little-travelled feet.

The doctor, practised in the limitations of science, was unwilling to allow fate to prematurely rob the footloose dreams of such a young life. Claiming the unquestioned authority of science, brandishing the sharp tools of his trade, the doctor severed and embalmed the boy's feet to the consternation of his mother. He placed them in a cornstalk raft, and with a firm push of his heel, set the float downriver to continue the boy's discovery of the world. The feet would touch lands far and wide, and who knows, perhaps even discover the child's father in the currents of the Atlantic where father and son ought to at last meet.

ON BEING POLITE

Out of breath, perspiring, anxious, rushing through the oldest quarter of the city, Lino moves as fast as his panic. His memory of the hideous crimes reported in that dirty district unrolls from his brain in a slippery carpet of terror ahead of his hurried steps down the cobblestone street. The river slows to a murky crawl. The cobblestone street undulates away from the riverbank and narrows to an alley. The afternoon sun stretches its long fingers, barely touches the deep walls. The alley waits steeped in shadow, and Lino expects gangsters at every corner, brandishing knife blades, and robbing him, or worse, stealing a prized part of his body. A kidney would be the obvious target. He has heard rumours that kidneys are in high demand on the black market. Lino eyes with suspicion a group of children who stop playing to stare at his frantic pace. He knows they too carry knives, a few even guns. Dark, unshaven faces loom by doorways. Lino hurries, determined, focused on the end of the street. The trick, he has learned, is to avoid eye contact. Such a small invitation to intimacy becomes an assured road to trouble.

Lino reaches the marble stairs climbing up into the next quarter. Relieved, he sighs. Parked cars sparkle against the turquoise sky. Houses, bright from recent paint and defended by gold-plated iron bars, stand proud, bordered by manicured lawns. His shoulders ease, his pace quiets and he congratulates himself on a safe escape. He promised himself never to be so stupid again, not to challenge his good luck. He hums, pauses by a gate where a budding camellia tree bursts into a bouquet of white hope. He slides his hand through the iron bars and snaps off a flower, placing it in his lapel.

A car horn honks. Lino turns, startled. A fair-haired gentleman steps out of a red Porsche double-parked across the street.

"I'm sorry. May I ask you a favour?" The gentleman loosens his tie and puts a jerry can on the ground.

"Certainly."

"I'm wondering if you would be so kind as to lend us enough money for a drop of gas to take us back to our neighbourhood. I realise it's a lot to ask, but better to ask than to steal, that's what my grandfather taught me." The gentleman adds a hearty, friendly laugh. Lino joins him with a chuckle.

He reaches into his pockets for change. Holding a few coins in his palm, Lino sifts through the silver to find a coin.

"My pleasure," Lino says, placing the coin in the gentleman's hand and turning to leave.

"Please don't misunderstand me, I don't want to sound ungrateful but I couldn't help noticing the other coins in your hand. They'll surely weigh you down on your walk."

"Weigh me down?" Lino scratches his head, puzzled. The gentleman grins.

"None of my business, of course, but if I catch anyone

stealing, I'll cross the street and punch their face to a crepe. We need a touch of civility in this city, you know. It gives everyone else a bad name. I've got principles. I'll have those larger coins too if you don't mind."

Lino glances at the people in the Porsche smiling back with a benign wave of the hand. He fishes a handkerchief from his pocket and dries the beads of sweat collecting on his forehead.

"People get hurt and everything. So unnecessary. There's enough in this world for everyone, don't you think?"

Lino, about to say something, hesitates, then the gentleman continues.

"No pardon for a petty thief. No worse sin I'd say. Never met a soul who'd refuse to share when they have more than they need."

Lino's outstretched hand, filled with coins, begins to tremble. He stares with a blank gaze at the man.

"Why don't you just hand over the rest of the coins before you scatter everything on the street?" the man says guiding Lino's hand into his suit pocket.

Lino's mouth opens but there is no sound.

"Do you have anything else that might help us?"

Lino nods his head, hand still wavering in mid-air, eyes transfixed, faraway. His legs quiver, threatening to fold. Lino leans on the iron bars.

"God will surely repay your generosity."

The gentleman returns to his Porsche, the smooth engine purrs and the car disappears from view, leaving the stench of rubber on asphalt lingering in the air.

THE PICNIC

After a lengthy search for a pleasant roadside spot, both cars screech to a halt and park underneath an inviting cork tree. Crumpled bodies emerge from the vehicles, stretch their bones.

Mr. Silva and Mr. Loureiro walk a few paces away and, with their backs to the traffic, piss in a long arc toward the blue horizon and the bright sunflower fields.

Mrs. Silva and Mrs. Loureiro haul wicker baskets in the opposite direction. Red-and-white tablecloths flutter to the ground, butterfly wings settling on grass. Glimmering silver pots follow, land with a thud on the chequered cloth. Pot lids open to reveal rice kernels sweating and steaming from the warmth of thousands squeezed together. The aroma of barbecued chicken permeates the air. Two of the children, hungriest, tear the newspaper wrappers concealing the chicken; in haste they pull the drumsticks, and voracious, bite into the flesh. For a moment, the sound of a cork popping from a bottle interrupts the chatter. The adults search for a glass to fill.

Mrs. Silva and Mrs. Loureiro sit on the edges of the improvised table delivering a convoy of plates. The children venture a little into the surrounding area and inspect the grass.

"Watch for snakes!"

The warning hangs suspended in mid-air.

From afar Mr. Silva and Mr. Loureiro admire the shine on their cars. Cars with which they spent the better part of the morning waxing and lusting. The intense summer holiday traffic continues to go by on the road. A few cars slow down to scout out the bucolic scene, seeking shade, envying the pristine luck of the picnickers. Magpies and sparrows, having fled the initial commotion, approach neighbouring trees in tentative short flights; their curious and shifty eyes examine the racket on the ground. The roar of an engine drowns the voices. One car overtakes another and grazes the ditch. An enormous dust cloud billows up. The birds fly away again.

"God dammit. Hope you're nailed to a tree trunk on the next curve," Mr. Loureiro yells and wipes his moustache, tossing the chicken bone over his shoulder. He curses the dull film of dirt settling over his car. "Pardon my language, Mrs. Silva, but that's what people who behave like animals deserve." Mr. Loureiro bows, touches his black cap with his index finger.

"Come here darling, don't talk to Mrs. Silva with grease on your mouth. Take this paper serviette," Mrs. Loureiro calls. A breeze steals it from her fingers and she is prompt to offer her husband another.

Shy, Mrs. Silva smiles and touches Mrs. Loureiro's hand.

"Ohhh ... Don't even mention dirt. Every time I've finished dusting my house everything begs for a wipe-down again. I've hired a full-time maid just to dust and scrub, but she can't keep up with the work."

"Ohhh ... don't be modest Mrs. Silva, you run the most spotless house I've ever set foot in. I would eat off your floor."

"Ohhhhh ... really!" Mrs. Silva does not hide her contentment. "We do the best we can, so help us God." She pats her lips with a paper serviette and tucks it under the table cloth. Manzé, come over here!"

The child, reluctant, approaches. Behind him, Manzé forgets the crumpled bag of chips he had been feeding to the ant's nest. A breeze spins it away, scatters the contents. The magpies and sparrows chase the bag rolling on the ground.

"What's this red dot on your chest?" Mrs. Silva stretches the shirt to her eye, then smells it. "Tomato," she concludes with a disappointed drop of her head. "Will never come off." She drops her arms in exasperation.

"Of course it will," Mrs. Loureiro encourages.

"Manzé, I warned you to be extra careful with the new shirt. Don't tell me I need to buy you a bib at your age. Do you think I've nothing better to do, do I have to police you?"

Mr. Silva and Mr. Loureiro crack jokes. After the first wine bottle sits emptied, they challenge each other's aim.

"Bet you can't hit the damn thing two steps away!"

"Ahh ... Can too. Can refill it blindfolded from twenty paces," he sniffs the air and adds: "And just by the fermenting stink of last year's crop." They laugh.

"The children, pleeeease," Mrs. Silva and Mrs. Loureiro protest in unison.

"All right then. We'll go back to stone-age games." Mr. Silva winks at Mr. Loureiro while crouching for a rock.

Manzé places the bottle a few meters away on a slab of rock. Men and children shower the bottle with stones. Serene, the bottle stands impervious to the taunting of stones and swears. Not dissuaded, small and large hands collect successive rounds of stones until at last, the glass shatters in a loud blast that unsettles the women and scatters shards throughout the vicinity. Everyone claims their stone the successful one.

"Mum, caca, caca!" Chico, the toddler, stumbles towards his mother biting his lower lip. Mrs. Silva grabs a handful of serviettes, picks up the child and heads behind the tree.

At the end of the picnic, tablecloths fold their wings, return to the wicker baskets, and the lazy, full bodies struggle to squeeze back into the cars. They leave with a screech of rubber on asphalt.

The magpies and sparrows return, dive for crumbs.

Cars slow down, scout out a pleasant lunch spot and pick up speed again.

THE SEMANTICS OF SHADOWS

When Severino interrupted his father's breakfast of black olives and red wine to complain again of missing the company of his shadow as he missed the best friend he had never found, his father Ernesto clucked at him with a slap on the nape. "Be thankful you are only missing a shadow." His father also reminded him it could have been far worse, considering Severino had been born through the mouth, following his mother's particularly indigestive meal of an entire plump chicken stuffed with boiled eggs.

"Who knows? Maybe there is more than a flimsy shadow to lose next," he added. A warning delivered to Severino, to silence his mouth in the event the bad omen might re-awaken and revisit the house. With a frown his father stared at the opened golden locket on his chest beaming a mini-ature sepia picture of his wife. "Remember, your mother was not as lucky." A stern half-finger wrote the reprimand on the frosty mountain air infiltrating the warped window sill, before he stepped out on his way to the quarry.

In his own mind Severino believed his rightful shadow had been stolen, sold out at birth to a greedy trafficker of influ-ences offering black market shadows to the many rebels desperate to slip unnoticed under the new moons.

The villagers in the granite enclave tucked under the mountain pass believed Severino a dead man already. "What living thing does not cast a shadow?" Ti Zeferino, feeding his donkey a handful of corn husks, pointed at the voluminous bulk shadow cast by his creature, and conveniently obscuring the just released dung pile. "Is this the smell of a shadow?" Severino asked, wriggling his nose. Ti Zeferino scratched his goatee. How could light not collide with this boy's body and spark the pool of darkness that everyone else did their best to keep one step ahead of? Ahead, only until the unavoidable day a person would slip into their shadow and embrace it in their burial den.

His aunt Laurinda, on a rare visit from the city, assured him the foolish envy of villagers reflected only the dimness of their words. "They covet your lack of shadow. A boy so pure, light travels through you like an angel. You are immortal." She left the smudge of her lipstick on his forehead, and he stared at it for hours in his late mother's wardrobe mirror, cherishing the blessing of his first mark. Although not dark as the shadow he longed for, the mark beamed its red and was the next best thing to a shadow sprouting from his skin.

From that day on Severino closed the wooden shutters in his bedroom. He retreated to the darkest corner under the paralysed arms of the grandfather clock. He sat in a rocking chair, ageing faster than the spider layering his cobwebs in domes of cloud-white threads suspended from the oak rafters.

With the flickering eye of an olive oil lamp for company, Severino disappeared with joy inside the covers of his books where he followed the trail of letters on every page, shadows of distant thoughts cast on the blanched emptiness of the paper. Those tiny intricate shadows of another mind cast wondrous worlds upon his own, and he was delighted to trade the unbearable mountainous winter fog he had been arrested in since birth for the limitless possibilities of other horizons.

Book after book, web upon web, storm after storm, he read every bundle of words kicked under the door by his father, who had resigned to supply this ration of sanity for a son already inhabiting another universe. Unbeknownst to Severino, always looking forward to the next page and hurrying after his thirst for knowledge, the books he returned had now shed the intricate shadows of their author's thoughts from their pages.

At first, Severino imagined it might be attributed to the mould of his lips as he shaped sound to each word. Perhaps he had sucked the words in with excessive voracity. That also might explain his lack of appetite and little requirement for bread and goat milk. However, even when he learned to read in silence, the letters still lifted from the paper and disappeared into his eyes as if their reason for being was fulfilled the moment they had been engraved in his mind.

After he finished the reading of each work, Severino now worried as the pages sat blank and soulless, the sign of a dead book. He blew out the olive oil flame and swung open the shutters. A torrent of light poured into the room.

It had been years since villagers had seen the light of Severino's eyes, so when they surrounded the window to peer inside his room and solve the mystery of his self-imposed exile, they gasped at the sparkling filament of cobwebs nesting a scattered flock of translucent book pages. The intricate filigree displayed the webbed architecture of one industrious in the art of imagining. Despite their scrutiny, the villagers could not locate Severino inside that room and soon abandoned the window. They overlooked the two blinking stars cradled in the arms of the grandfather clock, with its barren, numberless face still ticking the hours even if not moving a single arm.

When the night arrived hours later, the two stars escaped through the window as they lifted to the sky under the new moon cover, escorted by the fluttering pages also illuminating the skies.

UNNATURAL MIGRATIONS

Truth be known, I could be called a traitor. But I can't bear to remain silent while you are dragged away from your ancestral homes by the thousands. You, who harbour no sliver of hatred, falling to your knees, dignified, with no time for a prayer. If you could run, would you?

I admire your poise, standing proud. You are another of the forgotten races. Brothers and sisters breathing side by side from a time before *us and them*. My tribe cannot distinguish one of you from the next. You are the feared foreigners. I grew up with your darker cousins for my neighbours. Deep wrinkled skin, herded around the globe like slaves, you survive away from your native soil and thrive in inhospitable places, penned between the concrete of our cities. You build our houses without complaint. In our childhood we swing in your arms. Our hearts, our unrequited love, we tattoo on your skin.

I see you fall without resistance, without protest, least of all a shake of your head. You know our destiny is tied to yours. On windy days, I watch you dance, and hear you whistle intricate songs. I long to learn your tongue. You may think I'm crazy. I hug you. I see the scorn in my people's faces. My people see angels in the clouds, singing, and think it not strange. My people hear prophetic voices thundering in the sky, voices encouraging them to partake of the riches of the earth. Yet they fail to see you before their eyes. As if angels are only white, not ebony or ginger with green wings. Your land is only theirs. They build cathedrals. Adore. Saintly voices whisper everything they wish to hear, not what they need to hear. They pray to storms, and saints, and ghosts.

I want to know what you say. What you say to your young ones growing under your shade, the ones who will never reach your ripe age. I want to learn similar compassion toward my people. How you forgive us for using your daughters and sons to imprint our history and our gossip on their sliced hearts, bearing each line without a sound. As in this moment, where I tattoo my thoughts on your skin. How you see us destroying each other. Mad metal blades, murderous, swing in our parks. Hatred and greed bulldoze the rootedness that stands in our way. I beg your pardon for our lack of mercy. Our hunger comes from hell. The hell of not seeing beyond oneself.

THE DESTINY OF LITTLE MARY

The entire village called her Little Mary despite general knowledge the Holy Water of baptism had instead pronounced her Mary of the Sky. All along her mother had wished to name her Little Mary; however, Father Lucas, renowned in the parish for his inordinate obedience to the letter of the ecclesiastic law, insisted otherwise, unable to find in his book of names, the Bible, a saint dressed in such a diminutive naming. Thus, the menacing swing of his index finger refused to bless the newborn with the blasphemy of a name unwarranted by the Lord.

"Unmovable as Fortunato's donkey," people whispered, adding in resignation, "and no mind of his own, either." In this particular case Father Lucas had been offended by the attempt to belittle the sacredness of Mary, Mother of all, by the suggestion of such a plain adjective and, therefore, he refused to listen to village arguments in defence of modern times and fluid values. He further believed that a name opened the oracle of a destiny, that in reality he had saved the unfortunate child from being instilled with an irredeemable psychological complex. Furthermore, only one Mary proved worthy of carrying an adjective before her name, and in fairness he might have even entertained an exception and considered another more valiant adjective besides Little, as long as Holy and Sacred were safeguarded. At any rate, no one ever asked him for further views.

In truth, the child's mother, ecstatic by this blessing of creation, an only daughter after five attempts, and premature at that, was not naming her Little Mary to belittle the child, rather to state that her motherly eyes perceived her as a defenceless creature, indeed tiny, reminding her of a fragile dandelion gone to seed, a dandelion in danger of being blown apart by a simple breeze. She called her child Little Mary to remind every soul that even in the resilient casket of adulthood, upon pronouncing her name, her frailty would prevail and require extra precautions against the cruel world.

Spared the leather belting that her five brothers endured — often on her behalf — and sheltered from the hurricane of anger of a drunken grandfather, Little Mary grew up protected from the blasphemous tongue that tormented the boys, considering that her delicate ears would wilt at such indecency. The village watched with attention the unfolding of their delicate flower in the earthly garden, lending a protective eye from the moment of her first steps, extending their calloused hands and rescuing her from the impact of her falls. They watched her dreams gain shape as she entered the road of education to become the first village girl to leave for a destination beyond a convent or a distant husband's bed; and to return one day as the first woman doctor in the valley to practice among their kind. When the bus arrived to take her into her bright future, the village stepped out wearing best clothes, delivering hopeful speeches to wave her beyond the surrounding hills. Everyone's dreams and hopes also compacted in her suitcase, now heavy beyond her strength and requiring countless helpful hands to deposit it safely on the roof of the coughing bus.

Months passed until a telegram arrived to summon her home. Little Mary, in her innocence, was not aware that the course of her life had already changed. Her mother had died of a stomach ailment; a nastiness that had been spreading with deadly haste and hate, and perhaps since the day of Little Mary's departure. Village whispers blamed the knot of worry in her mother's stomach as the culprit. After the funeral matters, with the abruptness of any sensible response to an insensible tragedy, the governance of the family household fell upon Little Mary's shoulders. A title without a crown, a weight without a counter-weight.

Following this unexpected turn of events, Father Lucas walked upon the village cobblestones with his chest fuller and gait bouncier. In the eyes of the parishioners, he appeared both to have grown a length and shed a few wrinkles. In his sermons, he now invoked the perils of neglecting age-old precepts and rules. "In the sacred texts for a sanctified reason," he underlined with a flex of his eyebrows.

Villagers agreed they had been now demonstrated without a doubt that her diminutive prefix had affixed her to an unyielding fate. Little Mary had been thwarted from greater life achievements by the burden of her name, destined from the beginning to this foretold conclusion of pots and brooms, a far distance from the stethoscope and the prescription pad.

Aside from Little Mary's absence, Sunday mass attendance had again increased to historic levels. An elusive public sight ever since her return, Little Mary had nearly vanished in the whirlwind of the domestic demands, and in her mind it was as though the insurmountable hills surrounding her childhood valley had again closed in on her, settling the prospect of renewed dreams with the finality of a graveyard lid.

THE ART OF KNEELING

While her mother sewed the last button on her impeccable-white first communion dress, she decided to ask.

"Why don't men kneel, even in church?" she asked.

"Don't you have better things to think about, girl? How do I know the answer to such a question?"

Since first attending mass, she noticed the grave men, erect at the back. She noticed the women, devoted, folded over the pews, sometimes sitting, sometimes kneeling. She attributed the difference to etiquette. In buses men stand, women sit. Later, she attributed it to laziness. Women fall on their knees to scrub a floor, to wipe up a child's vomit and men stand, scratching their crotches, watching, tooth-picking.

"But why?" she insisted.

"Ask the priest in Sunday school."

"But mother, you have been kneeling for such a long time. You must surely know why!"

"Maybe because it's easier for us women, wearing skirts. We can kneel on our bare knees. The dust on those pews would dirty men's best pants and they would quickly wear out," she answered, snapping the sewing thread with her teeth.

Years later, she found the answer to her question while lying in beds. She found that men also folded in adulation towards their true yet unspoken version of the sacred, unable to stop invoking God, "oh God oh please God." She found them kneeling, willingly, in adoration, sometimes with their pants still on, sometimes not.

THE DROWNING

Beneath the sun's eye, in the centre of its spotlight, engulfed in the boil of panic, a man struggled to remain afloat on the lake's surface, his pleas for help muffled and interrupted by gulps of water. The man slipped below the waterline and surfaced in erratic intervals. His outstretched fingers, his fan-shaped hand, burst from the water, attempted to clench the air hovering above, teasing him. The hand sought the solid, any offering of support to hoist him above the merciless and unrelenting liquid, insisting to swallow his entire body.

On the shore, unbothered by the drama unfolding in the horizon, knotted in the lotus position, eyes closed, palms pressed and resting over her heart, a woman sat and faced the sun afloat in the sky above the lake.

As the wind, the loon, the trees stopped breathing and observed a moment of silence before the man in the lake, an old bearded man wearing khaki shorts and dangling camera, strolled down the forest path leading to the beach. On seeing the body struggle in the lake water, the man wasted no time in removing his sandals with a flip of the heel. He prepared to sprint when the clasping weight of a hand pulled him back.

"Come, come and sit."

"A man is drowning." The bearded man pointed at the continuous splash of white water in the lake.

"Sam is meant to be where he is meant to be."

The old man stared at the woman's radiant and calm face before he pinched his arm, the red welt widened, the pain shot up to his brain. The mark of his fingernails etched on his skin convinced him he did not dream. In addition, the pungent aroma of the lilac tree in the vicinity confirmed his wakefulness. In his dreams, he did not smell his landscapes.

"This man will die if we don't act."

"The world is perfectly imperfect." The woman sighed, shrugged one eyebrow. "Sam may die or Sam may live. No one can struggle on his behalf." The woman loosened her red tie, slipped off her ivory-coloured jacket. Her matching shirt caught the breeze and billowed. The pair of folded wings on her back fluffed up, unnoticed by the man staring at the commotion in the water.

"Don't be so hot-tempered." She pursed her lips.

A strange force magnetized the man's feet to the ground, his eyes to the woman's cleavage.

"Why am I arguing with you when someone is dying?"

The woman allowed her wings to flap open, drawing an expression of shock from the man. He scratched his beard. Hesitated, caught between his instincts and the apparent figure of spiritual authority before him. He wondered whether he would be wading in waters beyond his depth, were he to attempt a rescue of the drowning man when the professional rescuer appeared reluctant to do so.

The winged woman offered the man a bunch of grapes

that materialized from the palm of her hand. For a moment, he relaxed and sat on the rock next to her. At her insistence, he nibbled on a grape and watched the man struggle. Both the grapes and the drowning scene appeared real and tampered with his emotions: his shallow breathing soured his mouth. He had crushed a grape in his hand without noticing. Juice dripped on his legs.

The old man's eyes searched the edge of the water for a weapon: a stone, sharp, powerful, and capable of removing the nutcase from the picture, so that perhaps he could swim in with a tree branch, in time to save that man.

"Do not resist change!" The woman whispered, in her incantatory voice and to no one in particular. "It is a little wet and perhaps a bit suffocating, yet everything will quiet down in no time. I promise. All is well when it ends well." With closed eyes, hands pressed together, concentrated, the woman talked to an invisible interlocutor. "If you are struggling to stay afloat it probably means you are not ready to float. Don't force yourself."

"Why do you bother talking to him? He is struggling with the water and with himself. He does not hear you."

"Oh he does. I am inside his head. I am the voice in his conscience. I am the only voice he hears in this moment. The gulls crying above us, the breeze tangled on the trees, he hears none of that."

The man on the beach wondered what was more torturous, the struggle for breath and to stay afloat or the constant commentary of this woman inside the drowning man's mind. For the first time he wondered if indeed the man wished to die, if only to silence such an annoying voice.

The woman picked up a book, inconspicuous by her

feet, and opened it to the bookmarked page. The book was blank. She seemed intent on returning to her world inside the page.

"How can you sit impassive to his suffering?"

"Everything is perfect in our lives. If Sam accepts that fact he will not need to struggle, resist and agonize over these long excruciating minutes."

They both weighted her words against the picture of the struggling man.

"I must commend Sam on the choice of setting," she added, her arm sweeping the view as though for the first time unveiling the turquoise water, the white mountain peaks in the distance. "Breathtaking, isn't it?"

The man on shore twirled the ends of his beard as he watched with gritted teeth Sam's red hair skimming the surface of the water. For a moment, he wanted to believe his eyes tricked him and it was the sun itself that bobbed on the surface of the lake before it disappeared and sank. It was then that he also heard the woman's voice now in his own head: "Breathtaking, isn't it?"

He glanced over his shoulder, and found the winged woman nowhere in sight.

IV: AQUA LIBERA

ROBALO SILVA'S DREAM

Robalo Silva's imagination was boundless. From the time he was a fingerling, and to his teacher's despair, Robalo refused to immerse himself in school matters. In the afternoon heat, during their weekly field trip, and after the first eddy, he escaped the shallow waters, hiding behind a boulder.

Robalo Silva dreamed the impossible. His teacher disapproved: "It's been tried before. It can't be done, it's unnatural for a fish to fly," and with a clap of fins the teacher ended the reverie, nudging Robalo along. "Pay attention to the lesson, instead." The teacher's frown, etched on his forehead, reminded Robalo of the distant *V* of a bird in flight.

During recess Robalo stared at the faraway sun reflected above the ripples and dreamed of breaking through and flying. He began his practice. Awkward little leaps. His snout barely cleared the surface, yet he gained momentous glimpses into another world. Robalo's world distorted when he sank back into the current. The water, refracted and muddled. The narrow embankments, a confining prison.

In time, Robalo departed the placid waters of his childhood and drifted downriver seeking larger streams of consciousness. The years, the distance, the gulf between him and his origins widened. Only the unconscious pull of Robalo's migratory heart lured him back upstream for a yearly visit.

Attending a school reunion on one of his visits, Robalo Silva flapped his fins with passion as he detailed the progress of his dream. "Already half my body flies out of the water." Those who had long surrendered their dreams puffed their gills, saying, "He can't let things be. Must be different, thinks he is so special." Nonetheless, Robalo Silva believed fish would one day fly. He taught his two children, and later his three grandchildren to dream the impossible. Grandiose dreams required perseverance, lifted, push by push, by generations of efforts. Despite the sadness, he accepted with resignation that he, himself, would never reach a cloud. "My children's children will, their fins are already stronger than mine," Robalo muttered to himself or to whomever cared to listen. At the end of his life, in a courageous last effort, Robalo leaped above water for the eternity of a second. He died, as he dreamed he would, in the sky.

Generations and generations of Silvas, inspired by Robalo's determination, galvanised by his vision, pursued the dream of flying. Without realising when it happened, they found themselves in the air, fins grown into wings, thrusting them into sky.

The fish inhabiting the narrow stream had forgotten about Robalo Silva, the dreamer. They envied the strange feathery creatures, returning Spring after Spring to glide above their lives or dive, side by side, in common waters, as if a miracle offered them the key to both worlds.

How could these creatures move without effort between

air and water? The fish lamented their misfortune to one another. A misfortune shackled them to the bottom of the world, living shallow lives. In their prayers the fish demanded wings from their Gods.

On hearing the fish complain, the feathery creatures honked their encouragement. The fish did not understand. The fish believed the feathery creatures mocked them, and so they swam away, closer to the bottom.

To this day the flying creatures still shake their heads, ruffle their feathers, after they dive into a body of water and hear the fish swimming in circles, lamenting their fate.

EAU CLAIRE FISHING

A stone is not immediately a stone. Pebbles are accommodating, boulders are not.

Days, weeks, sitting by the river.

Nights stretched out on the river bed, rested on the pebbles' solid cushion. Days dreamed past me gliding the surface of the current. I whistled up thrushes. Howled above wolves. Fought for crumbs. Damn magpies. I argued stubborn ducks, until tired of quacking I skipped flat stones on the slippery surface. One day, I skimmed a pebble the entire width of the river. Imagine the feeling, imagine the puzzlement on the opposite shore. "Walking across the waters?" Sixteen leaps. The miracle of reaching the other margin. A thing of saints. I danced and a teary sky washed my face — who doesn't get teary with miracles? I was clean and they took me in.

"Dancing in the rain isn't a sane thing to do!"

I wanted to tell them I danced without stopping, two days and two nights, for that little pebble on the other side, the one that skipped across, that beat the pulling current, the surge of the stream.

"Howling at the moon is a lunatic thing to do!"

Luna mia. I wanted to ask if they were jealous, if that was why they've hunted down the lone wolves. I started wrong, started too loud and they clamped my mouth shut. It was a public park after all and after hours.

They pulled the straps tighter. I failed to co-operate, refusing the help, the generosity, from the concerned neighbourhood behind curtains. The neighbours, as always, lent a watchful eye, while I sat, suspicious, by the shore, this time bound, bound somewhere else. They shoved me inside the ambulance.

I cannot see the river through the whitewash of the walls. Diagnosed impaired. Cannot be solo, unsupervised, outside the institution. I welcome the blue pills, easier to dream of the river then. I'll pretend. I'll smile. Swallow every pill in the TV room. They'll be fooled. Is this what dogs learn in obedience school? Packs of nurses encircle the solitaire wolf. Round you up for life.

I'll buy a fishing rod, sit by the water, weeks at a time, staring, not at something in particular, everything in particular. People will notice the pole, line drifting in the current, their eyes unable to fish out the truth beneath the surface where the hookless line drifts, the peace of mind that glides downstream in the shape of an innocent leaf. I'm not in the business of tempting fish, but they, the people, hooked on the surface, hooked on the belief, hooked on the appearance, will nod, will approve, "Another fisherman," because they want to believe they know, they understand another mind, another river. Every criminal mind needs a motive, an alibi, just to be. To be left alone.

THE EFFORTLESS DRIFT

The current lures the trout downstream, the school misbehaves. Young trout flap belly up, in and out of the eddies, they enjoy the sudden thrust of moving water. The teacher admonishes transgressors with a nudge on the fins, pushes them to the safety of an eddy. A mixture of fear and excitement rushes through the young one's gills on this first excursion into the world of rapid waters.

Stories abound.

Older trouters in the class whisper frightening stories of a haunted pool, a quiet stretch further downstream, where many trout disappear in a veil of mystery. Food is plentiful there but after eating, trout spring out of water as if by magic, as if there is no gravity. It is said only the lucky ones are chosen, departing the waters, uplifted to the clouds. Some swear on their parents' scales it is a perfect world up there, heaven. Others swear the opposite, a world stranger and scarier than can possibly be imagined.

When Red Eye finds the teacher occupied explaining the origins of the moss growing by the shore, he tells of his uncle, a fortunate survivor. Young trouters surround Red Eye, their tails flicking with excitement.

His uncle relaxed in a quiet pool, watched the evening

news reflected on the pool's bottom, and absent-minded, nibbled on food fast drifting by, when, without warning he was hooked and catapulted out of the water. He gasped for breath. Strange creatures, limbs like reeds, attempted to snatch him, but he flopped in desperation, slipped off their hands and somersaulted into water. Later, on the pool bottom, still trembling, hiding behind a boulder, Red Eye's uncle espied the strange creatures who stood by the shore casting lines and skipping stones. When the sun floated away, they entered a silvery object and two bright yellow eyes spit light into the distance. The creatures disappeared in the swift machine, thundering toward the moon.

A splash of incredulity reverberates through the water, bubbles stream out of young trouters' mouths. Everyone laughs, uneasy laughs.

"Abduction should be left for science fiction," interjects the teacher who had glided without a ripple and joined the group, fins crossed over his chest.

The trouters, suddenly motionless and solemn, pretend they had been all along paying attention to the embankment and the botany lesson.

"Now Red Eye, let's hear what your uncle would say about the origins of the moss I just finished explaining," the teacher reprimands, tapping his tail on the water.

Then, in a splash, a worm falls from above, hovers in the middle of the class.

V: FORCE

PICKLED BRAIN

The horse-drawn hearse came to a halt on the cobblestone street. The animal's snort echoed along the grey stone buildings and sent the pigeons on the eaves fleeing in an undulating white ribbon.

Horace peered through the lace curtains wondering if the time had arrived for his next-door neighbour, a benign mind merely a week shy of ninety. A pity. Only yesterday, he had greeted the man on the front steps. A sprightly spirit and body carrying into his house his daily corn bread and goat cheese from the market down the street.

The driver hopped off the hearse, patted the face of his black horse, and offered it a handful of oats retrieved from his vest pocket.

Horace returned his attention to his breakfast of rye bread and a boiled egg, scribbling another corrosive note in the margin of the book he was reviewing for the newspaper. The knock on the door disrupted the rhythm of his methodic mastication and he nearly choked on the bread crust.

At the door, the undertaker greeted Horace with a little bow.

"My condolences, sir. We were told to collect the body of the man who did not resist the daily praise of God, despite his brain having been dead for some time. I am very sorry, sir."

"You are probably looking for Mister Nade next door."

The undertaker took a long look at the gold-plated numbers nailed above the door.

"One, one, five. This is the address I have been prepaid to collect the body from. I have been warned about the reluctance. I understand."

Horace felt the lump of egg in his stomach expand and press against his liver. He opened his mouth and nothing happened, aside from the burp smelling of improperly digested yolk.

A small group of curious people on their way to the market had gathered at the bottom of the stone steps and listened.

"This is the home of the literary critic with the nasty reviews, isn't it?" someone whispered.

Horace trembled. He slammed the door.

After that incident and every time Horace published a caustic book review, in which he had sharpened his witty adjectives into spears of nasty sentences, the undertaker would arrive with instructions to collect his body, even though in time he requested nothing more than his mind. In response Horace slammed the door on the undertaker's face. He had begun to grow infuriated at the predictable sequence of events, worthy of the most despicable cliché, and consequently he did not surprise himself the day his emotions overruled his analytical mind and he shot the undertaker in the mouth.

At his trial, Horace yawned at the unhurried pace of the proceedings and the redundancy of the questions. Inside the witness box, the faces of many an author grinned as they eagerly penciled their notes on the morose details of the case. Horace only shuddered on the morning of the sentencing when feeling the nagging egg from a rushed breakfast wobble closer to his liver again, expanding the pressure on the sphincter of Oddi.

Unsurprisingly, Horace was condemned to a prison sentence that would only be revoked when he authored a book which would receive unanimous praise from a jury of established authors.

On the second day of his prison sentence, the guards found Horace with his golden quill wedged into his heart, his torso folded over the open pages. The blood had soaked through every page leaving no white surface to accommodate even the smallest of prepositions. Horace had released himself from his last sentence.

The next day the prison guards summoned the undertaker to dispose of the corpse. The new undertaker, an author forced to undertake a new profession to feed his young family after the unwarranted and malicious review from Horace, hailed the hearse to a stop on the prison grounds. The man, who still called himself a writer, patted the black horse on the face, fed himself the oats from the bucket. Then, ensuring no guard's eye rested upon him, he fed the horse one more crumbled page from his vest pocket, a review from the deceased critic. In protest, the horse neighed.

Hours later, in a rain pour, unwilling to disguise his grin, the plainly-dressed undertaker returned in spritely steps across the rain-soaked grounds of the prison, undeterred by the mud slinging onto his trousers. Behind him, the sealed, rectangular box jerked and clanked in the wheelbarrow pushed by two guards. Although Horace's heart had been unsalvageable, the undertaker fondled in his hand the crystal jar in which Horace's brain would float and rest pickled for eternity.

A DANGEROUS GALAXY

I'm a dangerous man. I wasn't born dangerous, mind you. It evolved, a gradual process, following the hair tumbling down my back, beyond the confines of my shoulder, growing inch by inch, year after year, uncombed locks leading to many brushes with the law. I grew dangerous in subtle ways. My own folks wouldn't have noticed my criminal tendencies if it weren't for the people putting two and two together, fingers pointing at my hair creeping down my back, the five rings spiralling up my ears, the excessive, bright clothes — offending the sensitive eye. Sure signs of trouble.

I lived a peaceful existence, unaware of my obvious threat to public safety, until the day a gloved hand shoved me into a cop van for standing too long on one corner doing nothing. My head got in the way of the van's door and cracked open. The Force doesn't believe in star gazing. That's for Star Trekkies. "Interested in astronomy, eh! Carry any books on the subject to prove it?" Don't need to, I said, the sky, the subject, is right there, and I pointed to the obvious. I guess they don't like people pointing to the obvious. It's tough to be cop. Tough selection, dog-eat-dog sort of thing, only the smartest earn the right to a uniform. It doesn't suit everybody. They crack more heads than jokes. I explained that my silk tie stayed at the dry cleaner and my briefcase never left the office. "Sure, son-of-a-toke," they shouted. They booked me in and shaved my head. In the morning, they booted me out. I went back to the same corner in the evening. I don't like unfinished business. Halfway through counting the planets, better than sheep for insomnia, when another cop van cruised by, different guys, and kicked me in. They called me a skinhead. Too much hair or no hair at all. Hard to please the angels of peace. I asked them for precision, how long did the long arm of the law extend, because I had no intention of walking around breaking the rules. It took many centuries for the fathers of the nation to build such a great democratic country in wigs.

Insubordinate, disrespectful conduct towards an agent of the law earned me another complimentary night at the vomit hotel, breakfast included. "It's not the lack of hair, kid," the moustachioed cop reassured. "It's your face, your clothes. I only need to take one look at you to see you're up to no good."

I wondered if he meant the jeans, ripped at the knees, the tattoos, the pimples, the t-shirt saying Jesus was Left-Handed or the entire smorgasbord.

"Take this piece of free advice, kid," he continued, "Blend in and you won't find yourself in trouble. Ordinary citizens don't walk around like they have something to prove, like they're better than the rest of us working hard to maintain order." He marked tempo with the baton against the desk.

"These streets were made for walking, these stars were made to shine ..." I sang my version of the old tune my mother whistled to me as a kid before bed.

"Shut up. I don't want nonsense back!"

"But I was taught to stand up to nonsense, officer!"

And then the sky opened and I saw Draco and Orion's belt scintillating in my head, before everything became nebulous and I entered a black hole.

LIKE CORK AND BOTTLE

Doc, I don't know what to make of this child. She locks herself in her room. We worry. No sir, we remember no family history of anything wrong in the head. We're a tight, caring bunch, Doc, don't get me wrong. We sit downstairs watching TV, having a good time together. She refuses to join, penned in her room. I've peeked through the keyhole. She sits staring at the blank ceiling. Sometimes she draws on the wall. We can't have a brand new house destroyed with nonsense.

We locked her in her room after she hurled a pot at the TV screen and, lucky for us, missed. It's her brother's pride and joy. He bought it after he started working as a bricklayer for Justino. She and her brother used to be like cork and bottle. Now she just screams at him. The screams would be the least of our worries but you won't believe me when I tell you that she refuses to eat any food from the supermarket. She screams it's poisoned. It's all right, we tell her, it's packaged in nice plastic wrappings, see? I don't know what worm has gotten into her apple, Doc.

But if that isn't enough, she climbs out the window during rain storms. In the yard, she dances and dances, her long hair spraying rain as she twirls and twirls. If I didn't know her dance proved it a crazy thing to do, I would tell you it was a beautiful thing to watch.

No, she isn't hurting anyone dancing, but the neighbours come around to watch her, especially the boys, and we don't want our daughter to be in a circus. We're putting bars on the window.

All we want is for her not to make a fuss, just sit with us at dinner while we watch TV and eat popcorn like every sane person. That's not too much to ask, is it?

CROSSROADS

Screams and curses are heard first. Then, a struggling mother and her child enter the schoolyard's view. The determined mother, both hands locked around the child's wrist, drags the body of stubbornness through a cloud of dust.

In the schoolyard, the teacher stops welcoming grade two students, and their accompanying parents, and follows the latest pair approaching the schoolyard. The high-pitched wail of the child reminds everyone of a suckling pig smelling blood in the air, anticipating the butcher knife. The child, legs stiff, heavy as an anchor, carves a deep trail of resistance in the malleable clay.

The newly arrived mother empties a sigh of relief at the teacher's feet. She gathers strength for a last apologetic smile and stretches her hand to the teacher, half greeting, half begging for a rescuing hand herself.

"This is António, my son. He's all yours, Madame teacher!"

The teacher composes an obligatory smile and crouches towards the child.

"What do you wish to become when you grow up, António?" The teacher smiles.

António lifts one eye.

"I want to be a driver, Madame teacher. I want to drive a big truck."

"So António, you must attend school if you wish to be a driver someday."

"Don't need to, Madame teacher. I already drive my grandpa's big truck. He drives to Porto and I go along, sitting on his lap. I help him steer all the way. That's where I wanna be sitting, with my grandpa, travelling places, not sitting in there arriving nowhere." The child points to the sombre window where the sun does not enter the classroom. In silence, everyone follows the aim of his finger.

António, in a life or death alertness only desperateness brings, takes advantage of the momentary distraction, yanks himself free of the fisted chain and runs, runs, leaving his perplexed mother empty-handed.

The class, properly seated, recites the list of rules when António reappears around the curve, trotting in front of his father. The father marks tempo with the slight touch of an osier switch against his own hip.

It is only after António enters the class that the teacher notices blistered lines from the twig etched across his face. The father removes his black beret before stepping in. He holds it against his chest.

"It was a simple misunderstanding, Madame teacher. As you can see, António here arrived on his own two feet. He's very happy to be in school. Aren't you, António?"

António bites his lower lip and stares down at his

toenail, bleeding after a kick of frustration against an un-yielding stone.

"António, show some manners to Madame teacher here. She'll think we're savages without proper education."

António does not raise his eyes and the father gives him a nudge with the osier wand.

"Come on, tell Madame teacher how happy you are to be here."

"I'm very happy to be here, Madame teacher."

"Don't talk to Madame with snot hanging. You've got a perfect clean sleeve on your arm to give it a good wipe. Madame teacher might think all my children take after you." He twists the beret in his hands. "This one's taken after the devil or something. A mind of his own. Skin tougher than a toad's. Doesn't seem to feel, I tell you. At your service ..." And he departs with a slight bow of the head.

At the commanding nod of the teacher António shuffles his feet to an empty desk. The students follow the tap of the teacher's bamboo cane against the blackboard and chant in unison the sequence of vowels she points to, a e i o u. António sits staring at the blackboard, his ear attentive to the growl of a heavy engine rolling by.

THE KETTLE

"I am standing here before you, I don't know what I bring ..."

The radio slammed against the wall. Exploded.

On the thin drywall, a crater the size of a mouth swallowed Leonard Cohen's melancholic wail.

Nadine did not blink. Sighed. "There ... it's over now." She walked to the stove and turned the kettle on high. At the opposite end of the room Lee stared at her hands, then at the wound on the wall across from her. "One more voice silenced."

"Would camomile be all right?" Nadine asked, absently searching for a tea bag in the freezer. "It helps digestion." She brought out an ice tray instead, cracked loose the cubes into the sink. Realizing she did not need them, she turned the hot water tap on to watch the ice melt in the sudden heat.

"Pau d'arco would be fine," Lee whispered, still staring at the hole across the room from her. Her body slid down the wall and onto the floor. She cradled herself.

The curiosity of the shimmering moon, peering through the open window, highlighted the scattered pieces of radio in the unlit kitchen. Outside, arched backs and raised tails, hair standing on end, cats fought; their acute cries filled the room.

"Ouch!!! That hurt." Nadine hopped on one leg, lifting the aching foot to the cradle of her hand, dropping the tea cups from her hands.

"I'll sweep up the pieces soon," Lee offered. She twirled the engagement ring up and down her finger, continued to stare at the hollow mark on the wall.

The kettle on the stove began its noisy gargle.

"Damn it. For God's sake turn the lights on." Nadine bent down to pick out the radio screw that had stabbed the tender flesh between her toes. "The near future is dark enough, no?"

"If you can hear the music, why don't you help me sing …" Lee's melodious voice finished the interrupted Leonard Cohen song. She stared out at the moon, her fingers combing the absent hair on her scalp and measured the mix of ache and pleasure on her surprised fingertips, now missing the strength of her once red cascading locks, a signature of decades.

Nadine stopped searching the cupboards for another matching set of cups. She examined the room. Shadows stained every wall. The gentle sway of the bamboo blinds and the spider plant basket with its long droopy blades brought the only movement to the room. The shadows danced as a low growl exited Nadine's stomach. A muted complaint about the latest assault on the body during the torture chamber appointment in the bowels of a machine. All in the name of hope.

"Did you say something?" Lee asked. Her voice deep and tired as it always was even before the threat of any ending came to focus.

Nadine nodded. Shrugged.

The kettle steam peaked to a panicky whistle and filled the room. Neither Lee nor Nadine had the strength to turn it off, finding comfort in the kettle's rattling dance on the stove.

"Come." Nadine extended her hand, an invitation.

Lee accepted the life line lifting her up and she leaned into her embrace.

They swayed to the music of their memories, the voice of all silent fears in the song of the kettle's unending scream.

THE GOD OF SHADOWS

Messenger and executioner, understood and revered, there was a time I worked for the gods of suffering. Blessed by popes and ayatollahs, generals and priestesses, I was deployed, wearing the zest of a saviour, to bring the impudent down on their knees and report their reluctance to taste the worms; sent to expurgate stubborn cultures refusing to accept the light of change on the other side of reason.

I sigh for a misunderstood, bygone era, a time the depths of humanity proved worth my visit. These times of glory vanished with supermarket ice cream and the automobile, with every gadget and comfort that softened the body and wrinkled the spirit. Despite your contempt, a few of us remain. Only I carry on with the pride of my craft. I am the one you shake your head at during the evening headlines of horror. Night wanderers freeze, petrified, as they barely catch the flash of my silver signature of steel slashing through the dark before their last breath. The colour of life trickles down their neck, pools in their suprasternal notch; and, lounging on your sofa, you crave the description of suffering, mesmerized by the smell of pain, though you would not be caught watching in its vicinity.

I work the shadows, the shift of stealthy steps and echoes, to deliver suffering at the feet of those who fear pain, to those who vacillate between opening their chests and inviting the boiling wax or drowning in the syrup of pleasure injected in their veins. You should not waver when selecting the righteous path. The answer always lies past the shortcut, anything easiest and fastest. I do not take pleasure in the anguish I must deliver. Each time your body contorts in agony, do not despair, you are building the spiralling ladder that will lift you to the other side.

Only the fire of pain melts the crusts that cover your molten core. I have seen the eyes of gratitude in those who found themselves at the bottom of the world, among their excrement and tears, blood and broken teeth. Do not romanticize what I say, this is not a pilgrimage in your Adidas to Santiago, after which you hang your stories like precious stone anklets next to the pretty-coloured bruises and blisters that bring you centre-stage at any bonfire. Few cross the serrated peaks of their pain, having climbed over their broken bones to find the sea of calm in their minds. When I deliver those bodies to the other side of the divide, I stop, I can no longer help them. They have arrived. No burning iron, no nail-pulling will touch the essence of who they are. It does not matter what I do, their radiant smile illuminates their swollen eyes, it shines through the black and blue skin. They have transcended appearances and the frailty of the body.

I spit on the faces lost at the dead-end of alleyways, seeking my merciful delivery. They make me ashamed of my own humanity. Not even snakes flee flames with such expediency.

To the weak and the meek, I prolong their opportunity to save themselves, I offer a slow and excruciating redemption. I find these vermin most often among the filth of new-agers, that mob of belly-gazers, hedonists extraordinaire, who destroyed my planet, one bite, one wild remote adventure, one spiritual retreat at a time. They flew to their paradises of negative ions and positive thoughts, inebriated by spiritual feelings, blinded by the white light of good vibrations and sunbathing; the same excess of white light which decades later would also overheat the planet and melt their peak experiences of cool and would liquefy their mortal flesh without ceremony or blessing, without tarot reading or powwow, in the frigid waters of their daydream aquarium. I laugh at this tyranny of pleasure of the feel-good addicts. They believe there is nothing to learn in observing another's suffering. I laugh at this negligence. You must seek your own suffering to be saved. Remember Jesus? Delivered by one who understands the essence and the necessity of the most inconvenient moment. This is why I must inflict suffering. I gift us both the medicine of horror. Sometimes, I apologize for my lack of imagination. I cannot invent original paths to the garden of dread.

If you swallowed every word on these pages, you are braver than you imagined. Now, look down, way down, descend the slippery steps of your mind to where I am. The knot in your stomach. This is where we will meet after your last unexpected trip into ecstasy.

You will hate me or understand me at the end of these words. These pages reveal nothing about me and everything about you. What you feel as you read my words, will say everything about what you did not know about yourself. The discomfort you tasted will give you the piquant hint of the necessary strength for the day we meet.

So long, and be brave.

THE HUNT

Bow balanced on one shoulder, arrow bag swinging from the other, the man cushioned his steps on the loam of the forest floor. In the echo of his soundless motion, his young daughter followed his tracks, feather-light and un-noticeable in his shadow. On the trail, the man stopped and crouched to examine tracks on the edge of a puddle. He raised his head, rotated it from side to side, measuring the direction of the wind with his nose.

The man and girl crossed a clearing. Robins darted out of the tall grass and into the threads of thorny vines beaded with blackberries. A colossal shadow, gliding across the ground, startled the girl. She stared at the ground. The sunshine appeared to wash away the flash of darkness as fast as it imprinted itself on the grass. She looked up and followed the orbit of the eagle above the open space.

The man signalled the girl to sit at the edge of the clear-ing. The girl disappeared into the tall grass, harvesting an apple from her cloth bag. To encourage the offering of the deer's life, to make it meaningful to the creature, to give it a *raison d'être,* the girl had brought three apples to sweeten the sacrificial appeal.

Before they set out on their Fall ritual, man and girl had sung a prayer, painted their faces with the ochre of the earth. They asked the deer spirit to sacrifice its life for their winter sustenance. The man promised he would only kill the animal that offered a clear sign of surrendering. He would not use a rifle, he would hunt with a bow and arrow in the tradition of his ancestors, offering a better chance to the deer, an unequivocal chance to surrender its life to the wheel of creation.

The girl's first bite into the apple resonated through the clearing in a crisp crackle. The man frowned. The girl set the apple aside on her lap and opened a bag of raisins. Silent, sticky sweetness tinted the air. Distracted from their sky-patrolling task to warn the other animals of intruders, jays and crows swooped closer and closer to the bag. The girl hurled the sampled apple to the middle of the clearing.

Eager to play, the man awaited the game.

Through the corner of her eye, the girl followed the careful step of a doe on the opposite edge of the clearing, whose parabolic ears swirled, attuned to any unusual sound. The nose wriggled, tempted by the aroma of the cracked apple.

Bow bent and tensed at the ends, the man stood awaiting the doe concealed by a thick salal bush. The arrow had disappeared into the womb of the bow, only its tip showing, a sharp eye ready to dart.

Tentative step after tentative step, the doe reached the centre of the clearing, stopped within reach of the apple. A sniff, followed by the reverberating crunch of a jaw sinking into the red skin, crackled the air. The cry of an eagle scratched the indigo sky and startled the doe to a frozen stance. The man stepped out from his corner. Statuesque, the man and the doe stared at each other, part desire, part meditation. Meditation on their future, their past, on the wheel of creation, on the wheel of recreation, on cravings and desires, on meetings and departures. A meditation on all encounters and collisions that change life's direction.

Conversation and apple unfinished, the doe sprang into a run. The girl squeezed the raisins in her hand. The man held his breath for steadiness, did not release his arrow; instead eased the extended string, as though inclined to let the hunt go. With measured slowness, he pushed the arrow further and further from the frame of the bow, till the arrow came to rest with its lean and deadly length sticking out of the arch. The man waited — his firm and veined muscles held the arrow in place. He glanced at his daughter who smiled back, eager to understand the many mysteries behind the role of blood leaving the body to bestow life and death.

In swift and gracious leaps, the doe charged, resolute and doubtless in her trajectory to offer her life, impaling body on the protruding arrow. The arrow penetrated the doe's chest and her large, bright eyes steamed up with the warm trickle of red running between the hunter's fingers already caressing her face.

A crisp Fall silence wrapped the forest until the man and his daughter embraced the still-twitching fur and sang their first notes of gratitude, the unfinished red apple firmly clenched in the doe's jaw.

A NATURAL BORN KILLER

In his first attempt to hurt another, an unsuccessful story, the General threw his soother at the cat.

We laughed. Laughing proved not our best response.

He laughed back at us, dispatching a plate. He missed us, then made sure to remind us that his failed attempt as an infant did not prevent him from later becoming the most sought-after sharpshooter on the military market.

Before he could spell *die,* the General discovered his Papa's slingshot, and that signalled the last time Papa heard a sparrow in the orchard. The General stoned them clear, entertaining himself plucking the feathers from their half-numb bodies. When he started shooting pellets at chickens and cows, for absence of other moving targets around the farm, his Papa, passing on a family hunting tradition, pulled him into the autumn hills, where together, shoulder to shoulder, they chased the rare fox, wolf and partridge. A grand photo of an oversized boot on a wolf's head, his rifle pointing skyward, well above his boyish head, still welcomes every guest to his hall entrance. After he shot down every creature in the woods, he turned to the military for an unlimited licence to improve his deadly skills and a place where he found inexhaustible targets on every continent.

Solid. A steady eye on the target. Nothing made the General blink when his scope met the mark, not even that mother breastfeeding her child — the bullet pierced the infant's head before it lodged in the mother's heart.

A sharpshooter, his breath moved in invisible currents. Be it stone on a bird, pellet on a fox, bullet to the heart, or later when he became a General, a missile on a city — he loved the godly feeling of reaching beyond his reach, imposing his will across the sky. He pointed his finger at the world and decided who lived and who died.

Even after he retired, alone with his memories, and still experiencing the strength of his legs to carry him into the woods, the General consumed his days shooting road signs or windmill blades, old bottles and any occasional lost pet that crossed his scope.

Now in his advanced age and with house-bound legs, he spends his insomniac nights pacing the dim-lit corridors of his mansion, attempting to shoot down ghosts, their furtive, dead-faces following him, slipping from surface to surface on his one hundred and one house mirrors. One by one, alongside a grin of victory, he pulverizes every mirror, wine glass, and polished silver plate with his spray of bullets before he finally sits down to accomplish the most difficult task of his entire career as a sharpshooter. As he stares at the piles of glass fragments covering the floor of his mansion, one final mission remains to silence the last two small mirrors, which refuse to stop reflecting his past life, haunting his sleep. A smirk of satisfaction hangs from the corner of his lips when he raises each arm with the measured, unwavering hold that had defined his life. He then stares into the dark tunnels before his eyes, and with a sigh, pulls both triggers.

THE GOD OF SHADOWS: POSTSCRIPT

My son, remember:

You will suffer if you believe it is your divine right not to. Appreciate the blessing of birth. To be born, we suffer, the mother suffers; there is a reason, there is a necessity to break through, to tear and activate the nerve endings of being in order to arrive. Without suffering there is no arrival, the joy is mute. What has gone wrong in the arrival of a human on this earth and in this century? There are no more screams of pain in our birthing rooms. These soft humans arrive limp, their mothers sedated and emotionally absent, their fathers calm and smiley. What happened to the sweat-drenched and exhausted pictures of mothers who climbed the convulsing hills of birthing on all fours? What happened to the fathers, frowned eyebrows and gnawed fingerbone, dragged back and forth and farther along the fiery paths of anxiety, such disquiet branding their minds to the end of tomorrow, a disquiet that would never leave them for as long as their children survived them, the cry of their newborn denouncing a world filled with peril at the moment of fatherhood?

What mother do you know who will watch her child suffer and attempt nothing? There is none. This is the reason for the invention of fathers. This is the reason fathers encourage their children to step into the dark night barefooted. They understand that one day we all become motherless. Fathers understand distance, their children arrived from another body, the consequence of a distant desire and a fleeting scream long expired. That is the reason fathers suffer with their eyes open, watch a needle puncture skin, the knife split flesh, a fist occluding their sight.

Do not speak to me of love. Love cannot be distilled without pain; in the same manner bread cannot be made without grinding the grain to dust, before it will rise again. Have lovers forgotten it was the sharing of their pain, and not their pleasure, that bonded their love to eternity?

VI: FATHERS

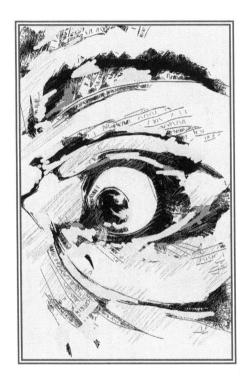

SUPERMARKET JUNGLE

He swings Natália into the grocery cart and slips her toddler legs through the slots. Natália's hands clap, legs dangle. As he pushes the cart, he notices the blur of flowers, the smudge of colour on the periphery of his vision, and this time instead of stopping and smelling the carnations, he hurries to the fruit section. Last time he stopped to admire the flowers, Natália, delightful smile and eager palate, anxious to swallow the world whole, plucked and chewed the daisies bare.

He pauses, decides to buy the local apples, in season, heeding the environmental warnings. His family may complain at home, but he is taking the Greenpeace article to heart. For the first time, he understands, loud and clear, what they are saying. He promises his best efforts to heal the planet. He vows to read through every label. "Do you know how many miles tropical fruits travel to please our spoiled palates?" He had argued with his father earlier. Today is the day he implements his new shopping habits. Local apples, that's it!

Can you believe what they do to bananas? The land, the poor land. The people, the poor people, paid miserable wages. Women giving birth to half-humans from the toxins and invisible poisons. Ashamed, he bites his lip. So long to hear their suffering. All that pain planted somewhere else, out of sight, and those cries of poison arriving from so far away they sound like a happy Chiquita banana commercial by the time he hears anything at all.

He drops the apples into a reusable mesh bag he remembered to bring along. Natália lunges from her seat, grabs a bunch of bananas. His fatherly instinct senses the movement and turns. Natália smiles, proud. A feat worth smiling about. Bananas are her favourite.

"Waaant, pappa."

"Way to go, cheeky one." He returns the smile.

He rescues the bananas before Natália bites into the skin.

"Oh ... no, no, no. Not this time, sweetie. Look, an apple!"

He holds the fruit in front of his child's eyes and pushes the cart away.

Natália cries. She ignores the dumb apple and twists in the cart without losing sight of what she must have.

Papa picks Natália up, brings the bundle of sobs to his chest and covers her in kisses, consoling. He tastes the salt, the pain. The crying gathers momentum with each step away from the bananas.

Cry. Cry. Cry.

Hug. Hug. Hug.

Other shoppers glare at his hopeless efforts to console. Bad. Bad father. Someone offers to buy the bananas if he cannot afford them. The child sobs. Natália's heaving chest sends shock waves to his heart. He smells calendula in Natália's hair, her breath, a sweet mixture of milk and innocence. He wonders what Mexican children smell like. Natália's cries pierce his ears and drown out far away cries, anywhere in the world. He remembers Natália's smile ten paces back. The most beautiful smile in the world.

He turns.

THE PLAYGROUND

He is a man among the see-saw of children.

A vacant swing rocks between intermittent cries, skinned knees. After a week in crowded apartments, the wound-up bodies unleash their appetite for running, jumping and tumbling. They signal their hunger to taste tears, laughter, blood. On purpose, for fear of vertigo, he avoids following the children's whirlwind and rests his eyes on a book.

Women huddle on a crowded bench. They do not return his smile. The day frowns, overcast. The women chatting among themselves, eyes alert for imminent danger, they shout periodic warnings to their children. Their don'ts, stops and be carefuls thunder above the breeze.

The commotion from the children's play sparks an occasional flash of change in the otherwise monotonous afternoon. His daughter rushes toward him, a cry above the playing swirl. She delivers him a scraped hand to be fixed. She nests in his lap. He closes the warm wings of his arms over her hiccupping body and blows on her wound. Blows with such fierceness the pain flies away to the upper branches of a poplar tree.

"Maybe going head first on the slide isn't such a good idea. What do you think?"

"Not now," she sighs, anticipating the reasonable, typical

lecture to be expected from an adult. Instead, she stares at the blood scratches in the shape of a spider web. She jumps off his lap. "I can trap flies now!" She sings, waving her fly-catcher arm in the air. A breath of wind puffs up her skirt.

"Would you like a sweater?"

"How will I feel the wind with a sweater on?" She shakes her head in disbelief and escapes into the twirl of movement, colour, erupting from the sandbox.

A stronger gust sends the huddling mothers marching into action, sweaters in hand. The children, forced into the wool, scream impotent don'ts, stops and be carefuls.

A mother, on purpose, detours by his solitaire bench. He opens his face in a smile. She does not.

"You ought to put a sweater on your daughter," the woman says in a sharp tone and stomps away, chin high, the wind puffing her blouse at the shoulders.

From the sandbox his daughter smiles and blows him a kiss. The man lunges in the air and catches the kiss with his baseball glove. He blows another one back, the kiss reaches his daughter despite the strong headwind, and she falls backwards on the sand from the kiss's impact, laughing without control.

REMEMBER AS YOU GO

"**I**t's bed time, children."

"Nooo, not just yet," they complain with the usual theatrics. Heads hide under the living room cushions, arms flail with compelling distress.

"Five minutes, then."

"Only if you tell us a story." The children scream in unison and beg, pulling on her sleeve.

The father, focused on the computer screen, emerges from his work. He notices the dark shadows around his wife's eyes.

"Give Mum a break, kids. How about I put you to bed and tell you a story?"

The room falls silent. The father hearing no, muffled under the cushions, looks helpless. His eyes plead to his wife.

"I'm fine, dear. Finish your assignment. I'll put them to bed." She walks over to him and runs her hand through his hair. He shrugs, as if saying, I tried. She smiles and with a hand-clap sets the room in motion. "Let's go, children. Come say good-night to your dad." She kisses her husband on the forehead and whispers, "I'll be down soon." He can tell her a story then. She waits for the children to embrace their father good-night and with a hand on the tiny shoulders she leads them upstairs.

The father returns to his work but his attention follows the upstairs commotion. Which pyjama to sleep in, repeated instructions to brush teeth in slow circular motions, no not to flush this time: "If it's yellow let it mellow," the mother sings.

"Is it Sleeping Beauty or Pinocchio, tonight?"

"Nooo ... We want you to tell us one of your remember as you go stories, Mum. Those are best."

Then, in a magical spell, the house falls silent and the father hears his wife's soothing murmur. He walks to the staircase and sits on the last step listening.

"The gigantic sunflower, with the gentle nudge of the wind, bent down to better hear little Narciso.

"Hello, beautiful flower. I'm Narciso Esquecido from the desert city of Leyte. I've walked this far in search of the sacred waters of remembrance."

The sunflower smiled and shook its wide leaves. A sweet shower of pollen sprinkled Narciso.

"Hum ... I see," said the sunflower. "You must ask the Admiral butterflies. They dance and twirl, kiss and hop, from flower to flower. They see everything. If you ride on the back of their wings you'll see the world from side to side."

Her lilting voice lullabies even the grouchy refrigerator motor quiet. For a moment, they seem to hold their breath, listening to Narciso Esquecido's first flight on the back of a butterfly.

At the end of the story the children clap, begging for one more. The mother explains that stories flow like honey and honey should never be harvested all at once. A beehive stores sweetness to nourish in the bitter cold of winter, so should the words of stories. The children do not argue with her.

The father returns to his computer. The screen-saver travels through space and into a black hole. The night ahead promises to be long. After his meteoric success, winning a national prize, a prestigious literary magazine awaits delivery of another of his inspired stories by morning. He begins anew.

"The gigantic sunflower ..."

GOING OUT

"I'll be darned. I heard you two started going out!"

My father does not mean he is surprised we are out on the beach boulevard walking hand in hand. He means he is surprised we actually began fucking, licking, kissing, stripping our clothes off and off and off, roaming over the territory of our bodies, waves of thirst, tongues surfing the rolling flesh, crab-like hands crawling in the salty mist, and the spray at last.

"We are not going out. Not just out," I assure him.

I mean, we have been going in and out, in and out, slow and delicious and slow. Yes, going out of myself, and into another world.

"Ohh ... You two aren't just seeing each other, you must be more serious than that, eh? Tying the knot?" My father looks puzzled.

Again, he is surprised we are not just seeing each other with our clothes off, feeling each other for what we truly are, after months and months sitting in a café across a sea of tables, watching, imagining, the torture of never seeing through what needed to be seen, until we could not bear the torment and with courage, she swayed up to my table to confess she would love, she would love to see me ... unwrapped!

There is no braver soul in the world than the one who asks for the truth. In awe, I peeled my shirt, baring myself bit by bit, until the server clearing his throat pointed to the sign:

NO SHIRT, NO SHOES, NO SERVICE.

So I tell my father everything he truly wants to know but did not have the courage to ask. He blushes. He does not expect the truth, the truth being the hardest gift to receive, the truth, bare, beneath layers and layers of veils.

As he buttons up his long winter coat, up to the last button and over his throat, I imagine my father's body beneath the layers, I imagine, before he rushes away flustered, without a farewell kiss, the way he, like most, run away from the skin of another man.

THE FLASH

I killed my daughter. How will a father
explain such
a moment? How will I look at these
murderous hands
that carried her death sentence. I remember
her blue eyes, pleading
to free her, while my hands clasped her wrist,
my hands forced her to die
before my eyes. Just like that, one moment here, the next
limp, limp as a platter-bound sole.

And the hate in my wife's eyes. The love in her
words assuring
it wasn't my fault but the
will of god
striking our
family.
I killed our child. Nothing will
disguise the loss,
the suffering.
God does not exist.
There will be
no forgiveness.

Everyone knows I killed her. My
daughter
knows I killed her. I saw it in her eyes. While I
dragged
her from the Bugs Bunny morning cartoons
against
her will. On the excuse of the approaching thunder
storm,
we rushed hand in hand to fetch eggs
for lunch, and carrots
for Bugs. She kicked and
screamed
like she was being
taken
to the electric chair. I told her
to
be quiet or else the neighbours might think we were
killing her.
She screamed "You are," wiped her tears and without
another word
followed. In my pocket
I hid
the weapon, like one who hides the
truth between the lines.
Her mother asked what was with me. Why the
urgency
to take our daughter, peacefully staring
at fantasies.
I whispered to my wife the plan. I winked.
She should
have stopped me at that moment. She smiled. She did
not guess everything.

Outside the supermarket I invited my daughter
on the coin operated
bee. Cartoon music blared. The bee searched for her
long lost father.
Other kids loved Maia, the bee. My daughter did not.
She preferred the red automobile.
That's what she glued her eyes on
when I suggested
with a persuasive squeeze on her wrist to climb on
the bee's back.
She protested again, this time without
shedding a tear, as if
saying you truly wish to kill me. Brave, she climbed
to her death,
biting her lower lip. Her yellow dress
matched
the stripes on the bee. Her blue eyes drinking
the light,
colourful sprinkles of yellow, blue, red. I fished
out the Polaroid.
She cringed, afraid of the flash. My
parents, patient, had waited,
for her photograph in the dress bought for her at
Christmas.
Their anniversary approached. Proud,
I smiled. I told her
to smile too. She stuck her tongue out
one last time
and screamed to get her
off. I pointed the camera
the flash went off as

her body
fell limp on the floor as if she had been
hit by lightning.
At first I yelled at her to jump back on
mercilessly,
for spoiling another picture. Then, I noticed the burns.

Everyday I carry this washed-out photo I will never send.

HISTORY LESSON

Repeated shaking awakens Manuel.

"Five minutes to get dressed, washed and out the door. No time for breakfast now," the voice echoes in Manuel's head, distant as yesterday.

Outside, wind argues with trees, rain hammers against the window pane demanding to be let in. Manuel does not bother to open the blinds. The sun will not rise for another hour. He growls at the start of another day.

"Every morning the same damn story, Manuel. When will you be responsible for getting to school on time?"

Manuel jumps into yesterday's clothes, barely wets his face and doesn't bother to brush his teeth. On his way out the door, he grabs a bun with butter and races to the bus stop.

"You forgot your gum boots and umbrella—" he hears his father's voice drowning under the drumming of rain on asphalt.

At his desk, Manuel nests his head between his palms and struggles to keep his eyes open. His shoulder aches from racing to the bus stop with a loaded knapsack bouncing up and down, leather strap jarring a bruise on his collarbone. His feet in wet sneakers, cold shivers up his spine. In secret, he wishes he caught a terrible illness. Then, he would not be expected to attend school for a day, maybe even days.

The teacher reads the lesson outline, "Child Labour in History." The students yawn in shifts as the teacher turns away to write on the blackboard. Intermittent coughs and sneezes from the class punctuate the teacher's speech. Only an occasional drop gliding down his still wet hair and falling onto his nose startles Manuel.

"Can anyone give me a contemporary or even a historical example of child exploitation?"

"Factory work in Asia."

"Very good. Any more examples?" The teacher writes the answer on the blackboard and, resembling a caged animal, paces from wall to wall. Manuel doesn't have the energy to shift his head and waits for the teacher's body to return to his field of vision.

"Roman slavery," another voice tries.

"The British coal mines," a yawning voice mumbles.

"Very good, very good," the teacher nods pleased. "Back then children were expected to contribute their share of labour to the community. They had to learn adult skills."

The classroom does not respond. The air, musty, dangles heavily from the ceiling. Manuel entertains himself guessing when a particular drop of condensation will fall, and on whom. The few windows do not allow the feeble winter rays to penetrate inside. The artificial light hurts Manuel's eyes.

"Do you realise how fortunate you are to live in a country that eradicated child labour, the progress we achieved since the brutality of the dark ages?"

In silence the class stares at the teacher.

"What would you hate most if you were a child in the coal mines?"

"No time to play!"

"Being away from home!"

"Not seeing my parents all day long!"

"The darkness!" says Manuel.

"No fresh air!"

"That's true. Children worked hours under miserable conditions. Often they wouldn't see daylight and their health deteriorated, vulnerable to innumerable diseases." The teacher shows a drawing of a child holding a pick axe beneath a lamp hanging from a cave ceiling. The teacher continues. "Unfortunately, in some countries, the status of children remains a far cry from the rights and privileges that we enjoy here. Instead of attending school and getting an education, children labour alongside their families in the fields. As for cities, they work on construction sites or in factories, long hours, exploited and ..."

The bell rings, interrupts the teacher's sentence. Feet shuffle. The cascade of snapping Velcro and the slamming of bags on the desks fills the classroom.

"Before you leave I want you to read the next chapter on capitalism. Also, write three pages on child labour," the teacher yells as they race for the door.

A collective moan erupts above the stampede of feet.

For lunch Manuel eats cookies and chews gum. He sits by an iron-barred window, one of the few windows in the school. "Having fewer windows reduces vandalism," he heard one teacher explain to another after a series of attacks and break-ins. Manuel gazes out the window, looking for the hills. His view, trapped by black clouds, stays confined to the maze of cement walls.

During the last class, darkness arrives again. Expectant, Manuel watches for the headlights of the school buses crawling in slow motion through the schoolyard. The bell rings and the last stampede of the day echoes in the corridors.

Manuel arrives home, exhausted, and watches TV until dinner.

His father forces him to move to his room after dinner to finish his homework:

"This is when you should be cultivating good habits and a work ethic. The future starts now."

Manuel drags his feet up the stairs, mumbling a protest under his breath.

Manuel falls asleep on his desk, leaning over the school books. His father switches the lamp off, carries him in his arms and tucks him in bed with a tender kiss on the forehead.

REAR-VIEW REFLECTIONS

The car radio newscast announces the outbreak of another war. On air, live, for the time being, a distinguished panel of political commentators analyses the inevitability of this particular war. "Give war a chance," one says. "It's in our blood, we simply cannot stop it," a second adds. "The human race has been warring since time immemorial," concludes the last.

"Be quiet, John," the father yells above the crackle of voices.

The father worries. Will he be sent away? How many people will die? Will he die? Will they lose everything they own? Should he drive back to say good-bye to his parents?

"I'm warning you, John. If you don't stop singing and bouncing I'll dump you out on the highway. That's a promise."

John does not misunderstand the ultimatum, the threat in his father's voice, the bottled-up fear spilling over in anger. Frozen, John sits in silence for the next five minutes. Restless from half a day trapped in the death seat, and before he realises, he begins his nervous singing once again.

The car stops with a screech of rubber on asphalt and John, grabbed by the scruff, is thrown into the ditch. The car pulls away.

The father glances in the rear-view mirror and remembers with a sudden tightening around the heart, similar waving arms and screaming in panic after his father's black Ford on the eve of WWII.

The political analysts agree it is too late to stop the war.

The father slams on the brakes.

AN APOCALYPSE OF STILLNESS

In the west skies, collected in an apocalypse of stillness, clouds gather in mourning, awaiting the sermon of the wind that will instigate their march toward me. In minutes the rumbling of an immense, indisposed belly echoes along the celestial corridors of the prairie prompting the end to formalities. In motion now, the storm stains the cornfields with its capricious mosaic of shades while crows and ravens flee on a diagonal course over our red tile roof, on course for the woods on the north side of the farm. The robins follow, destined also for the shelter of the oak foliage.

Yesterday, my father would have called me from his room above the porch pointing at the darkening sky, asking whether any tools lay forgotten in the yard and needed saving from the approaching baptism. We would both laugh. Yesterday, the kitchen window ajar would have allowed the cool shift of air a passage, and we, breaking cornbread at the table, would have smelled the storm before the static electricity lifted the hairs on our forearms. Then, we would have exchanged glances understanding that sooner or later clouds clashing over our heads nearly always deafen our beliefs.

A moment ago a third celestial flash illuminated the silence of a distant argument only seconds away from arriving in my ears. The rage and the fluorescent rip in the sky confirmed the absence of amnesty. The rips and the shouts are inseparable. The wind now slaps the apple trees in the yard, they bow in respect and accept the inevitable. Those to fall will fall. There will be no argument. The cornstalks in the field also kneel, thirsty and weary from the golden week, from promises now fulfilled.

Without yet a saving face of raindrops on the dust of the yard, I anticipate the moisture licking my palms, softening the weary skin, and I raise my hands to the sky in supplication. The wind ripping the oak foliage crowds out all thoughts and even birds have swallowed their songs.

The raging rain falls with the determination of the self-righteous, at last sinks its arrows into the earth. The urge to run in the yard and dance, spin and spin with the grass, blown and tossed with the leaves scattered in the yard, overtakes me.

Struck by lightning, an oak tree creaks, undecided whether to kneel or to stand in face of force. The burnt smell of bark occupies my nostrils. That is not my will. I look toward my father's bedroom window. The sound escaping the window almost resembles a last moan.

A frail cobweb links the veranda railing, the light bulb and the vase of gladioli. Frail, almost invisible, except under the exact angle of changing evening light, the web billows in the gust. The spider arrives for a hasty evaluation of her installation and scurries away to the safety of a curled ball and a muted rant. A last minute mending, perhaps. The pearls of rain whipped to shape by the driving rod of wind, finally enter the porch. The rain pelts my bare feet and stings my shins. I do not move away even when the thunder breaks over the roof, shaking the porch. The rocking chair does what is expected. It creaks.

The window in my father's empty room swings open and through the night bangs against the storm. It is a consolation to hear the argument of wood and glass against the forces of nature. I do not stop it. I am still rocking on the porch chair when the sun rises and erases the storm with the blink of its drying eye. The breath of the morning leaves a trail of cold down my neck, seeps into my chest. A familiar, earthly perfume populates the motionless air. A conclusion to the argument has arrived.

MISUNDERSTANDINGS

The happy fly dives toward the man, grazes his head. Concentrated on the crossword puzzle, the man throws a lazy and disinterested sweep of his hand toward the general vicinity of the annoyance. The fly rubs its legs, mocks the man, being too juvenile to understand he is not the patient type. Next, the fly loops around his ears. The man ignores the annoyance, wishes the buzz away.

The fly returns in acrobatic twirls enjoying the play. Young and reckless, refusing to be ignored, she lands on the man's nape and pinches his flesh. The man jumps. He slams the pencil so hard the tip breaks and the newspaper tears. Annoyed, his focus disturbed, he points a silent blameful finger at the creature now walking upside down on the ceiling. No one, absolutely no one, interrupts him without paying a price; the usual remedial smack.

The fly continues her acrobatic flights until she collides with his wavering arm and becomes entangled in his forest of curls. The fly shakes, spills laughter. A wing rubs another wing. The persistent buzz of wings irritates the man, who stops paying attention to the indecipherable crosswords. He freezes and waits with the patience of a predator. The happy fly, puzzled, crawls up his arm. She stops, saddened. The playtime appears over.

The man's eyes target the fly. Nothing in the world exists apart from the nuisance. The swing of his arm falls with meteorite strength.

Lying in the cradle at his feet, the baby begins to cry.

THE ILL-FATED CORNER

Narciso Sisudo ascertained death awaited him around that fated corner. He was convinced of this, since last month, on his way to the Conservatory, just before he passed the door of the ice cream parlour at the corner of Rua da Assunção and Avenida dos Ascenção, his heart staggered and he capitulated to his knees.

In the hospital bed, staring at the ceiling, Narciso Sisudo considered himself fortunate, blessed by divine intervention, having stopped short of that ill-fated corner. Content with the forewarning, thankful for the privilege of a second chance, he intended to be on his feet as soon as he could convince the doctor he was fine and that he would heed her serious words of advice, "Stay away from steak and gelato. Don't cut corners, it's hard work to stay alive!"

He would also promise the doctor that on his way to the Conservatory, he would choose the longer route, the one by the vegetable market. The ice-cream corner was ill-fated, he agreed.

At last on his feet, Narciso Sisudo walked with a slight tremble in his legs, a burdening knowledge that his days were numbered. When he found himself at the mouth of Rua da Assunção again, Narciso Sisudo, leaning on a cane, peered down the crowded street and espied Death lounging around the ice-cream parlour. Death stood out from the masses in a neon-green spandex outfit and a fluorescent orange tie to match. Colours Narciso did not recognise from childhood. From afar, he observed Death, patient in temperament, dawdling, lighting cigarette after cigarette, leaning on the arcade pillar, waiting for the unaware to trip on its step. Narciso Sisudo realized that once Death established an appointment it would wait, if need be, a lifetime, but most times not so long Death would linger at habitual corners, recognising the victim despite the shelter of a crowd, certain that sooner or later creatures of habit succumbed to routine.

A month later, despite his mind's protesting thoughts, his body led him down the street, diluting him in the tide of people flowing along Rua da Assunção, carrying him in an effortless drift.

Narciso Sisudo observed the hurried faces beaming youth. Immortal and only looking forward, they reminded him of his life until then. He built a name for himself. In all likelihood his name would survive beyond his flesh, memorialised in the spoken breath of people yet to be born. His music would enter their ears, touch generations of hearts long after his fingers had ceased to crawl the piano's unending staircase. His body would turn to dust, then wind, and later return to music as wind rustled leaves and serenaded lovers in the night. Fame and a little fortune were the price. *"A man of intense sensitivity, a refined human being, his music would move you to tears, inviting you to experience the entire spectrum of human emotion,"* critics claimed.

His music had long moved his family to such depths of emotion they fled across the Atlantic and never returned. First his son, then his wife, swam away in a crescendo of tears. Narciso woke up one day, high and dry, stranded on the island of his own self-absorption; he woke to face the morning Waltz with the decrepit chair where he sat to write his symphony scores. Narciso Sisudo's passion revealed little more than his obsession in disguise. The music in his head had drowned his son's pleas to take him to his swimming meetings, while his sensitive ears grew deaf to his wife's desperate invitations for countryside walks or a trip to the sunny islands. His refined sensibility failed to hear the growing staccato in their voices. In the far corner of his house, behind the locked door to his study, he entered the labyrinth of his torments and produced the much praised *obra-primas*. Inside himself, he discovered an entire universe of sounds, populated by his notes; and with the generosity of time in his hands offered his musical gift to the world.

A few paces from the ill-fated ice-cream parlour, Narciso Sisudo imagined his funeral procession overflowing the city streets. A complete orchestra followed the casket, performing his world-famous requiem. Admirers crowded his coffin, shed tears, hurled their arms in the air hoping to touch him. He did not recognise a face, except for the neon-green arm tossing him a rose from a distance.

Acknowledgements

In their vast majority, the sudden fictions in this book were written between the years 1994 and 1999, and concurrently to my first book, *The Scent of a Lie*. Both books share between them several characters who desired a longer life, an extended voice, beyond the bounds of one sole narrative or book. Many of these stories also began to be first published in literary magazines as early as 1998. I am delighted to have finally encountered a publisher willing to support the form of sudden fiction and now offering you those narratives collected in this book. I would like to thank Guernica Editions and their editors for their rare literary vision.

I am indebted to a number of first readers who generously gave of their time and whose fine eye helped these stories grow: Nowick Grey, Jim Prager and Lucy Nissen.

When the spotlight shines upon those standing on the public stage, there is often someone steadfast in their support, yet far shyer, standing beside the curtain, blowing them kisses. A sweet thanks to you, Heather.

It takes a village to nurture a storyteller. A heartfelt appreciation to you my friends who have nurtured and encouraged me on my literary path. There are too many of you to name. You know who you are.

This book is also for my friends and family of yesterday, today and tomorrow. May you find your own misfit, oddball, geek, rebel, eccentric and outside-the-box thinker selves ... and fear not.

For financial assistance during the completion of this book, I am grateful to the British Columbia Arts Council and the Canada Council for the Arts.

I would also like to thank the following Canadian and International editors as well as their magazines and anthologies in which some of these stories previously appeared in English or in translation: Prairie Fire, Whetstone, Café Irreal (USA), LitWit Review, margin (USA), orange, Saskatchewan Naturally, the-phone-book.com (UK), SAAL — Saber Suplemento (Azores, Portugal), dANDelion, filling Station, existere, per contra (USA), Neo (Azores, Portugal), Shelf Broadside, Ripe, Ópio (Portugal), Voz do Caima (Portugal), Esquina do Mundo (Portugal), Seixo Review, Stand (USA), Tesseracts 20 and Write.

About the Author

paulo da costa was born in Angola and raised in Portugal. He is a bilingual writer, editor and translator living on the West Coast of Canada. paulo's first book of fiction, *The Scent of a Lie,* received the 2003 Commonwealth First Book Prize for the Canada-Caribbean Region, the W.O. Mitchell City of Calgary Book Prize and the Canongate Prize in Scotland for the title story. In Portuguese he has published a collection of poetry, *notas-de-rodapé* (2005). His poetry and fiction have been published in literary magazines around the world and have been translated to Italian, Mandarin, Spanish, Serbian, Slovenian and Portuguese. For more information, go to: www.paulodacosta.com